THE CAT AND THE HOLIDAY COTTAGE

BY

Leona Day

Book 1: A Cats and Cottages Romance

TABLE OF CONTENTS

CHAPTER 1

Every morning at six, Larry would climb onto her hip, purr, and start making biscuits.

Amy might not have requested this kind of alarm clock, but she grew accustomed to the pressure of the cat's paws kneading her middle as she slowly awoke. As soon as she touched his fluffy belly, however, Larry would hop off and peep his resistance, giving her a few precious minutes to snooze.

The cat had entered her life as a skinny orange kitten, meowing by a recycling bin behind her office. He had walked right up to her, confused and hungry, the bell on his collar jingling, and she had taken him home. The internet posts and fliers Amy had made had done no good: over time, she concluded that the cat was hers, most likely abandoned by the family who had given him a collar and little else. It made Amy sad to think of someone abandoning him, but she appreciated her loving Larry, who had grown into a sturdy, perpetually hungry best friend.

She even appreciated the early wakeup call on some mornings. Larry was only trying to help, giving her back some of the love she gave him.

After three years, they had developed a routine: Larry trying to trip up Amy in the kitchen, plotting to make her drop the turkey for a sandwich she was preparing for her lunch, Amy sweeping Larry into her arms when he was on a mission to listen to birds, insisting on cuddling his orange fluff instead. A loving, flawed relationship like any other.

As she picked up Larry later that morning, he let out a crabby "yaaaaonnnng" of dismay. "Oh come on, Larry," Amy coaxed, "it's gray outside and the coffee isn't ready yet. Give me some of those purrs."

Larry settled into her arms, his arms dangling, offering a creaky, grumpy meow.

"What do you say we bargain, Mr. Larry Cat?" she reasoned. "Let me sleep until seven-thirty and I'll let you be until nine. Oh, you don't like that? Then snuggles it is." Amy heard the click of the coffee maker finishing and carried Larry into the kitchen. He jumped down from her arms and hopped onto a small metal stool that was just the size of his ample bottom.

Taking her floral mug down from the cabinet, Amy paused to shake off some of the cobwebs of sleep. The brightening morning sun had started to peek through the row of trees in front of her apartment. It was one of her last days here before heading north to Virginia, to the lake. She pushed the stress back inside her mind, just for a minute longer. She knew the view of the lake cottage would help, as would seeing her mother; today, though, it was hard to ignore the Italian coffee maker Conrad had used to make them coffee, his Florida Marlins coffee mug, and the last of the artisanal coffee beans he used to love. He had left, but his things gave her pangs of regret.

Her heart sank, remembering. Larry thudded down from his perch and nuzzled the back of her calf. Animals really know when we need them, she thought. "You're right, Larry. Time to start the day." Amy poured her steaming coffee, booted up her laptop, and settled into her favorite chair.

No work just yet, she thought. It's time to warm up a bit. She logged into her favorite crossword puzzle website to see what today had to offer. As she clicked "enter" to see the puzzle, she heard her other alarm clock ringing.

"Hi Mom," she said, picking up the phone.

"Good morning, sunshine!" her mother called out in a sing-songy voice. "Two more days! Just checking to see what I can pick up at the store while I'm out today. Glorious day out here."

Amy smiled in spite of herself. It did feel good to be cared for. "Nothing special for me. I'm using an almond milk coffee creamer for coffee lately, but I can pick some up on the way. How's the weather been up there?"

"Mild in town, but you'll want to have tire chains for when you're up at the lake cottage. I wish you'd just stay in Haverton with me."

"Mom, relax. Larry and the other cats will be a bad mix, so we really should be at the cottage, especially for longer visits." Amy's mother, Rebecca Guillaume, had been adopting and fostering cats for decades, and always had at least six semi-feral cats and kittens figuring out their lives under her roof before they were adopted into loving homes. Larry did not do well with chaos, kittens, or change, so the lake cottage it would be.

Her mother's words were muffled at the other end of the line. "I know, I know." She paused, eating. "Sorry, just having a scone. Ugh, dry."

"Sounds like you need some jam and cream. Or at least some tea or coffee!"

"Thank you, Amy, you can keep me in line when you get here. How long did you say you would be home?" Rebecca laughed at her daughter's attempt to "fix" the situation.

Amy paused. She didn't know how to respond. Would it be too much, being at home, seeing her high school friends happily married while she was newly alone? Or would the quiet lake comfort her as it always had, so she could work remotely from the cottage, cuddled with Larry and planning her next move?

"At least through the new year. Can I bring you anything from Florida? Some citrus?" Perhaps being purposefully vague was a good idea.

"I can make a grapefruit cake if you can bring some up. We can talk more when I see you." Rebecca's tone fell a bit. "I'm just a little worried about you."

She shouldn't be. "I'll be fine." Eventually. Someday. "I'll fill you in, but I need to get going—" Her voice caught at that last bit.

Maybe it was too much for her already.

*

Things were definitely too much at Arroyo Plaza, where Amy was trying to shop for both Christmas and her trip north. There was not a parking spot to be found, and Amy circled the lot until she saw one spot open up in the very far corner. The organic grocery store would help her with the few items she needed to bring up to the lake, including Larry's favorite chicken crunchy treats, so she would start there. South Florida didn't seem especially festive during the holiday season, but Amy had adapted over her years there, and found ways to enjoy herself and appreciate the twinkly lights even if Christmas mostly meant t-shirt weather, ocean breezes, and crowded parking lots.

It had been twelve years since Amy moved to Miami for college, pursuing a degree in marketing, and landing a coveted internship at the largest television shopping channel in the country. She had worked there ever since, and at thirty found herself second-in-charge of overnight programming. It wasn't daytime programming or prime-time, and she wasn't running her department, but she was proud of what she had accomplished so far She could work remotely for weeks at a time, she wasn't blamed if inventory failed to sell as expected, and she made enough money to pay her bills. Her dad used to say, "there's more to life than money," and "always know your worth," and she tried to fit in somewhere in between.

When she finished her shopping, Amy crossed to the neighboring Royal Thai restaurant and found her friend Lyra already waiting for their dinner date.

"Hey, friend!" The tall brunette with the broad smile gave Amy a hug. "Love your hair."

Amy patted her recently-highlighted light brown hair. "Thank you! It was time for something to cheer me up. I'm feeling pretty done with Miami. Done with these guys. Done with a lot."

"Good for you! You've been hiding out for too long. Do more things for you." Lyra ordered some spring rolls and drinks for the table. Amy was already feeling more relaxed. She really did need to socialize more. "So what's next? You sticking around for Christmas?"

Amy sipped her mai tai, and helped herself to dipping sauce for her spring roll. "Nope, going up to see my mom, and bringing Larry."

"Ouch, that sounds a little bleak. Larry's great, but you need more to look forward to in life than your mom and the cat and a bunch of dead leaves or whatever they have up there. How long do you have for vacation?"

"It's pretty flexible. Why, what's up? Are you traveling?"

"Nah. I'm sticking around and going to my mom's. But for real, we need to get you on with your life, see some new humans. I know you don't love to go dancing, but we've got to think of something. You've been so lost since Conrad. Let's do a long weekend or something, find somewhere all-inclusive. I'll be your wingman and we'll see how many heads we turn."

"I feel like I'm in a good place," Amy lied. "But thank you." Why didn't she want to meet people? Conrad had moved on. "And I just want to turn one person's head. The right person."

Lyra rolled her eyes.

"No, not him! Not Conrad, just— whoever I meet, I don't want to waste any time on someone who isn't right for me."

"That's not how it works—" Lyra began, but the conversation paused as their rice noodles and curry arrived at the table. "—oh yum, this looks fantastic. You need to give people a chance, let yourself feel a connection. Don't reject something that hasn't even been offered." Amy nodded. This made sense. "Anyway, what about Cabo?"

"Cabo?"

"Cabo San Lucas. Mexico. There's a ton of resorts, good-looking guys travel there, and we can ride horses on the beach. At least come with me so I can have fun. Hmm?"

Amy thought about it. It did sound fun, maybe for a few days in the middle of her visit home. Mom could help with Larry, and Lyra was right—she would have actual fun, and she could afford it, especially with a roommate chipping in. "Okay, I could get into that for a few days. And just to show you I really am over Conrad, you can have that baseball mug of his from my place."

Lyra clapped her hands together, grinning. "Love my Marlins! Leave it to me. Just send me some dates and I'll work something up for us." Lyra would have made a fantastic travel agent in the days before the internet. She loved to plan, which was marvelous for her job teaching high school algebra. The job paid horribly, but Lyra loved it and her students. Plus, her wealthy father had paid for her condo so she had more disposable income than most teachers. Amy knew she could trust her friend to find them a great little getaway, and plan all of the details perfectly.

Driving home, Amy realized she was actually looking forward to the holidays, to the trip with Lyra, to seeing her mother. Her rosy lips slowly spread into a smile, a genuine one. Being single felt so vulnerable, but she had people she loved. She imagined peeking inside her stocking on Christmas morning, something her mother still insisted came from Santa Claus himself. There was no ring in the stocking this year, but there also weren't any expectations.

This burning torch she carried for Conrad would extinguish…someday. Perhaps she could even learn to see him at work without tearing up at what could have been. "I'll be fine. I hope."

CHAPTER 2

"Peppermint Latte for Amy!" Amy reached forward and picked up the tall white cup with one hand as her other slid the warm drink into a cheery red sleeve.

She sipped the hot, vanilla-mint latte right away. Yum. This would definitely do for the first leg of the drive. She shuffled through her phone for the right playlist and found it—"Merry and Bright"—just the thing to start the long holiday drive. "You ready, Larry?"

Behind her in his travel case, the fluffy orange cat grumbled. He hoped they were not bound for their usual driving destination—the veterinarian. Larry was not a fan of wellness visits.

A jazz version of "Jingle Bells" started to play. Larry's grumbling settled down. And they were off. There were two weeks until Christmas and Amy was ready to dive headlong into the season.

The drive north grew cold gradually. At first the weather seemed to be getting better, but then the chill set in. Amy's wavy, light-brown hair, frizzy from the Florida humidity, actually started to relax as she drove north. She noticed that her hazel eyes stood out more without the mane of hair distracting her. She saw sadness in those eyes, yes, but also hope. For his part, Larry slept, curled up like an orange donut.

The sun went down by the time she made it up to North Carolina, and Amy really wanted to speed the rest of the way home just to get the night driving over with. It was such a long drive, and there was still a lot of road left. She disliked night driving because there were so few sights to see, and she began to yawn from boredom. As much as Amy loved Larry, the cat had no idea how to play Twenty Questions or the license plate game to stay awake.

As Amy pulled over for a break, she checked the temperature indicator on her car. 45 degrees! Brrrrr. She hadn't seen a day that cold in years. If I can handle Miami air conditioning, I can handle this, she reasoned, and pulled up at a gas station, in pursuit of a hot drink for her and a treat for the cat.

*

The door to the gas station opened with a "ding" announcing her arrival. Amy wanted to be in and out as soon as she could, because Larry was sleeping in the car. Rationally she knew that a sleepy cat, covered in fur, could handle a slightly cool evening for a few minutes, but she still worried about him.

It wasn't much of a store, and it smelled a bit stale, but there was a large coffee station along the back wall, with a few different self-serve blends. She read the descriptions, trying to decide.

"Viennese and Sumatra are the best ones here—" the voice came from behind, startling Amy. It must be an employee, she thought.

"Thanks," she said, looking behind her. "The employees dress well here, don't they?" she asked, realizing her mistake as soon as the words left her mouth. "Oh, you don't work here. So sorry!"

He laughed. "No, but I've tried all their coffees, so I guess I'm the next best thing. I drink a lot of gas station coffee, you see."

Amy laughed in response. "You sound like a real connoisseur." Well-dressed, clever, and handsome. And tall, with thoughtful brown eyes.

"Don't tell anyone. Really. I wouldn't want the praise going to my head." He grabbed a cup for his own coffee, enjoying the banter.

"So, um, you like the Sumatra, then?"

"Yes, it's one of my favorites here." He continued to smile, perhaps letting his gaze linger too long on her uplifted face. She blushed and looked back down.

"Um, well you've sold me, I guess," Amy said, filling her to-go cup. "Hope this gets me through the end of my drive."

"You have far to go?" he asked.

"About three hours."

"Ooof. I feel that. And it's no fun at this time of day. I'll leave you to it, then. Drive safe!" She and the stranger parted ways.

That was fun, Amy thought to herself. She should try out her chatting skills on handsome men more often. And of course it was harmless, some short banter with a local who drank a lot of gas station coffee.

Smiling, she settled into her car, catching up on texts before she was back on the road, Larry munching a piece of turkey from a children's lunch kit.

To Lyra, she wrote: "you'll be proud of me! I flirted with the hottest guy at a gas station in rural North Carolina." To her mother she wrote, "three more hours. Might just go directly to the lake cottage and sleep. Is heater working there?"

As she was about to drive off, the phone dinged once more. "Just turned it on—should be nice and toasty for you! Love, Mom." Her mother always signed her texts.

Amy settled in for the home stretch, her cup of Sumatra yielding tasty and spicy flavors as she drove on.

*

Every recognizable landmark in Haverton gave rise to wonder as Amy drove past. It was all as she remembered it, and she felt like George Bailey rediscovering his love of home in her favorite Christmas movie, *It's a Wonderful Life*. Her old high school and the converted water mill down the road pleased her the most. As children, Amy and her friends used to climb down beneath the mill to play among the rocks and the stream. During the winter they would admire it after snowfall. The mill had definitely had a recent glow-up, with a new coat of red paint, bright white trim, and restored stonework. Amy made a mental note to drop by for a visit. She didn't spend a lot of time on social media, but the mill would make a pretty picture to share.

Amy drove through Main Street and reached the edge of Haverton, turned off the stereo, and concentrated as she took the winding road up to the lake. Tall pines flanked each side of the road. Amy knew the trees were rugged and sharp, but their lushness seemed calming and soft to her as she drove.

The nature here was different from the tropical climate she had learned to call home. There wasn't snow yet, thankfully. Amy had missed the cardinals, the deer, and the changing seasons. She could have a fresh mango and date milkshake any day she wanted in South Florida, but a quiet pine forest on a misty morning was something else entirely. This change of scenery was just what she needed. And the fresh smell of pine and the chill in the air were comforting indeed.

"You have reached your destination—" announced the car's navigation system. Amy pulled over and parked on the right-hand side. There was no house visible, just an old mailbox and the top of a wooden stairway, but she knew her way around. Ooof, those stairs. Not looking forward to that. I must have blocked the memory of them, she laughed to herself.

First thing first: the cat. Holding Larry's travel case carefully in one hand, and her phone-turned-flashlight in the other, Amy tackled the stairs. There were thirty of them, all wood, and fairly steep, winding all the way down to the lakeside cottage with its gorgeous view. The air was lovely and crisp. Larry did not appreciate the extra motion and growled softly. Amy remembered with sadness the time her grandmother had taken a partial fall down these very stairs, and had to move in with her mother, leaving her lake cottage for good. It just wasn't safe to take that risk after a certain age. Even at her much younger age, she'd have to be very careful unloading the car, because some of the stairs were in desperate need of repair. Maybe she could help her mother find someone while she was at home.

The tiny wooden cabin with a bright blue door, however, had been built to last. Amy grabbed the hidden key from its place on top of the door frame. "This is us, Larry." She opened the door, to the familiar smell of old wood and old linens, the smell of generations and happy memories. Her soul needed healing, and this was the place to heal.

*

Twenty minutes later, Amy caught her breath. There had been six trips to the car, keeping loads light because she didn't want to lose her balance. Boy, she never wanted to look at that cumbersome suitcase of hers again, but she had to admit it was good to get the difficult part over with.

Larry had been hiding out in his carrier, sniffing the house and getting used to the space. Now that Amy was down and settled, he emerged, sat upright, and looked directly at her as if to ask, "what are we *doing* here?" He opened his mouth as if to peep, but no sound emerged.

"It's okay, Larry-o, you're on vacation. You'll have so many birds to watch and things to smell that you won't know what to do with yourself." Then he sat on his fours like a small loaf of ginger bread, feet tucked up, looking calmer.

Amy curled her legs up under her on the sofa and let her eyes wander. There was the impractically large stone fireplace on one side of the room, and the wall of lake-facing windows opposite. She remembered sitting at the little table by the windows with her grandmother, using her crayons to draw pictures of all the flowers in grandma's garden. She had used all of her reds because there were so many geraniums.

Now, there was no one home but her, but it felt so unchanged and so welcoming that she began to tear up. The old braided rugs on the floor, the gaslight that had been turned into a table lamp—even the silly vintage saloon doors that led to the main bedroom—all of it was a home she had forgotten, and now realized she missed dearly. She had been so lucky to know this and have this. Not just one home, but two: a special one by the lake, and a small home in town where she could walk to school and to see her friends.

What awaited her back in Florida? She wondered whether she could even have the family she wanted. There was nowhere as comforting as this, and it seemed there would be no one to share it with her. But Amy knew better than to let these thoughts get the better of her at night. It must be time to rest. Time to head through those saloon doors.

As she turned out the bedside light a few minutes later, Larry hopped up onto the king-sized bed with Amy. "You feeling better, little man?" He twitched his tail and flopped down next to her. "That's a good idea. Time to rest."

Chapter 3

"You're really here!" Rebecca crushed Amy to her, smelling her daughter's hair like she had since Amy was small. "This house hasn't been the same without you."

Amy looked around the house, mostly unchanged since her last visit. Mom had a fancy new pressure cooker they had discussed at great length, and she had finally taken down that old yellow landline phone with the twisted cord, but other than that, it was cheerful as ever.

"Eeeee?" She looked down to see a tiny grey foster kitten introducing himself.

"Well, hello there, what's your name?" The kitten walked around in a little circle, then stepped forward to sniff the tip of Amy's suede boot.

"We haven't named that one yet—he just arrived yesterday. We think it's a he. I'm so glad you're here—I've been running out of names for them! We get a hundred or so a year between the three of us."

Mom and her two best friends called themselves "Crazy Cat Ladies," but they were just kindhearted retired women who wanted to help every stray they saw. Amy knew that those kittens had helped save her mom after they'd lost her father suddenly a few years ago. Having something to love and help –that was a lifeline to Rebecca.

Amy crouched down to look at this little gray fluff ball. He sniffed her hand, and peeped again. She couldn't resist holding him, and picked up the nearly weightless creature. He purred loudly from the excitement of it all. "Let's see, what should we name you, you handsome charmer?"

"We just had a Smokey come through here. That's a good name for a gray cat, but haven't thought of anything for this one yet." Rebecca found Amy's favorite coffee mug—large capacity, with a faded teddy bear on it, and poured her a cup from the pot.

"Let's see. This one likes to join the party, and he's a little cuddle bug." Amy petted him gently, and the kitten started to doze. "Could you put some of that creamer in it?" She nodded her chin at the bag she had placed on her mother's counter.

"Almond and coconut milk? That actually sounds pretty good. Think I'll try a splash myself."

"What about Ash? Do you like that, little one?" The kitten was snoozing quietly.

"Ash is good. I think it suits him."

Amy smiled.   She sniffed his head, feeling the bits of gray fluff tickle her nose. "It's hard to be a kitten these days, isn't it, Ash? So many naps to take, so many purrs."

Her mother reached forward to transfer the kitten to her own arms. "Don't let your coffee get cold; I'll put this one in the kitten bed to snuggle one of the others."

"How many fosters are there now?"

"Just the four. Three and their mother.   The mother is gorgeous—long-haired, all black—and super sweet. I'd keep her myself, but my hands are full with this bunch."

Amy poked her head around the door to the living room, looking for the mother cat, but didn't see anything. She looked around the room again, slowly, remembering how little it had changed. The television was bigger and flatter now, and there was a nest of charger cables on a table by the front door, but the roomy, comfy sofa was the same, and the fireplace, with family photos framed on the mantel, remained just as she'd remembered. The table where her dad used to work on crossword puzzles, the afghan they'd huddled underneath while watching all those

Winter Olympics. Amy had good parents, and in this moment she felt so grateful. Whatever life handed her, she always had someone to help her come back from the edge.

Her mother held up a filled notepad. "There'll be plenty of time to relax soon, but we have a busy day ahead." Oh boy, she thought to herself, that looks like a long list.

*

It was a list of people in town Amy hadn't seen in years, and her mother wanted her to take the whole tour. They started at a local café, where Luann insisted Amy just *had* to try the breakfast burrito, and next they were off to George and Honoria's tea shop where a massive scone appeared in front of her before she could say a word in protest. Amy didn't know how much more hospitality her belly could handle, but everything tasted so fresh and homemade.

Amy groaned as Rebecca's station wagon pulled into the Larsen Nursery parking lot. "There isn't any food here, is there?"

Her mother chuckled. "I think we are safe here. Just trees and greenery. No edible plants."

It smelled divine, the crispness of pine and spruce. "I'm starting to feel a little Christmassy after all, Mom!" She patted her mother's shoulder and both smiled as they entered the nursery office.

"Hello, ladies!" Mrs. Larsen had aged a bit, but her rosy, cheerful cheeks were just as Amy remembered. "Amy, you look just like your mom!"

"Awww, thanks, Mrs. Larsen. Merry Christmas!"

"Thank you, sweetheart." She was like Mrs. Claus with her red-and-white apron and little round spectacles. "So what can I get y'all today?"

"We need a 7-foot tree and a whole bunch of greenery! I'm decking the halls while Amy's in town."

Amy looked out at the lot of lush, full trees. She clicked on her phone camera and captured the view—it was lovely now, but it would be a winter wonderland when the snow came this weekend. She really was glad to be home. The drama of Miami and Conrad was far away, and there was nothing but peace here at home. Amy started thinking of kind things to do for her mother— picking up Chinese food, helping around the house, maybe even hosting a dinner at the lake cottage. Then she wondered what Larry was up to—sleeping, sniffing, or watching for birds. She was so lost in her reverie that Amy didn't notice the man pull into the parking lot or approach Mrs. Claus, er, Larsen.

"Hey!" came the masculine voice. "Coffee girl, right?" It was the man she'd tried to chat with at the rest stop—what was he doing here? Amy gasped, her cheeks flushing.

"Hello—I'm, um, surprised to see you here."

"What does he mean, coffee, girl? Amy what did you—"

Amy interrupted her mother. "We just met when I made a stop on the way up here. This nice gentleman recommended a coffee blend to me." She held out her hand to shake his. "Amy Guillaume. Sorry, I don't remember your name."

"Vincent. Roth." His hand felt warm and rough on hers. And big. "Just got into town—you from around here?"

"Sure am. What brings you to Haverton, of all places? It's great, but it's a little sleepy around here."

Vincent opened his mouth to answer, but Rebecca interrupted—"You should show Vincent around, Amy. Give him your number!"

It was Amy's turn to open her mouth, but in shock. "Mom! Sorry, forgive our friendliness. Haverton's a very friendly place, as you'll learn."

Vincent smiled at her awkwardness. "Nothing to forgive. I grew up in a small town, and I know the way things work. You moved away, I take it?"

She nodded. "I live in Miami." He whistled. "Yeah, I know, it was a big culture shock."

"Lots of big houses in Miami—love to check it out sometime."

"Well, I don't have one of them," she laughed. "It's just me and the cat."

Oh great, she sounded like a loser—alone with a cat in a city full of nightlife and decadence. Nice going, Amy. She couldn't remember wanting to impress someone like this, at least not recently, and here she was stepping on her own toes.

"I mean Miami would be nice for work," he explained. "I'm a real estate photographer. Mostly luxury estates. Travel all around Virginia and North Carolina."

That actually sounded interesting. Who was this guy? "What brings you all the way out here?"

"There's some big lakeside estate that's going on the market, and they want to have some offers in by Christmas. I'm picking up some branches and things to help stage the photos a bit."

"Oh right, there are a few like that over there. What a cool job!"

He smiled. "Thank you! Actually, would you mind giving me your number? I can probably find my way around okay, but I'd love to pick your brain for recommendations since I'll be here for a couple of days."

Amy couldn't help but grin. Oh gosh, I must look so awkward. "Um, sure! Here, I'll text you so I know who's texting me." She looked at her phone so as to avoid more blushing.

"Don't worry—I won't abuse the privilege."

"Hey, it's the least I can do when you helped me choose the right coffee to get me here."

"Sumatra's my favorite—just had a cup this morning." Their eyes met. He was a little older than she'd thought, with a bit of gray salting his temples. He seemed to be searching her eyes for something, and she looked away, flushing in spite of herself.

"Well, enjoy the town—text me whenever and I'll help with what I can."

Amy and Rebecca packed up the station wagon while Vincent went off in search of photo props for his shoot. That was a clever staging idea, Amy thought. People loved to think about celebrating the holidays in their dream house.

Her mother drove home with a smile on her face. "He's a handsome one! If you won't go out with him, maybe we can convince him to take a couple of the kittens—"

"Mom! You are impossible." She laughed. Her mother and friends were responsible for almost all kitten rescues in three counties. "Maybe he has a giant, terrifying dog."

"Nah, I don't think so. He's not the type. And he likes you, and you have a cat--"

"I think he's just extroverted, Mom. They're among us, you know." That was probably it.

"You're an extrovert!"

"Mom, we are sitting here driving home and I keep thinking about when I'll do my online crossword puzzle so I don't break my streak. My crossword puzzle streak." Definitely not an extrovert. The idea of curling up with a warm drink and a crossword—and maybe even a purring Larry—was just the right idea for a frigid night like this one. She wondered if the snow would come tonight. It was getting chilly, especially when the sun ducked behind the clouds.

"I miss that grandkitty, Larry. Maybe I'll run out there tonight and scritch those pointy orange ears."

"I do need to pick up a few things before I head back to the cottage. Want to come by for dinner? I can make something easy to eat and pick up a bottle of wine."

"Oh, I'd love that! No one's cooked for me in ages. Cook anything at all!"

The two bid goodbye so Rebecca could feed the kittens and keep them out of mischief—and give their poor mother, the fluffy black cat her mother had named Midnight, a break. For her part, as much as she loved this time with her own mother, Amy wanted a little peace and independence.

*

Amy opened the cottage door to a peevish Larry, who yowled his displeasure at having been left for far too long.

"Oh, you poor thing! All alone all day."

"Mraaaaaap." Larry trotted around the kitchen as Amy unpacked the groceries, his tail twitching. She found his treats and rewarded his patience.

Amy checked her phone for the time. Hmm, four o'clock. Catch up on some work, cuddle Larry, then make an easy dinner for mom. "Ow!" Larry had pounced on her toe. "Message received, sir. I will return home earlier next time. Needy little thing."

"Peep?" He looked up at her. That fluffy little orange face.

"Come here, you." She scooped him up in her arms and went to the window. The skies were clear, and they looked out together at the calmness of the lake. This was where she needed to be. Larry settled in to the snuggle, enjoying the security and the view. It did feel good to be home. If life involved pain, the people who knew you and wished to comfort you eased the pain. Amy didn't want to stay in Miami, having to go in to the office and see Conrad, so smug and happy with his new girlfriend, and she couldn't start over somewhere new—she couldn't bear to explain herself to strangers over and over again. This was a perfect place to be, at least for a few weeks.

She remembered that she had Vincent's number and thought about texting him. He seemed to want her to, but she didn't know what to ask or say. Larry hopped down from her arms to hiss at a bird. She opened her laptop instead. She still had a job, after all, and it was a Monday.

Almost instantly, Amy wanted to close her laptop. There were over a hundred new messages that had come in from 8 to 4. Oh, this was not good.

The shopping channel where she worked had a cutoff for holiday shipping that was fast approaching. Any issues with inventory were linked to her role in charge of overnight programming—if they didn't have items to ship, then the schedule needed to be adjusted. This time, a shipment of travel cribs had been delayed at customs, and the "family travel" hour of programming she had scheduled needed to be rethought.

"Those cribs were supposed to be the highlight of that hour! What do we do…" Amy had made the excellent suggestion to sell more child and baby items in the middle of the night, when mothers were awake and nursing their babies. It had been a successful programming decision, but what were they going to do in the absence of a key item that had a high profit margin? Think, Amy, think, she said to herself.

She logged into their inventory database, hoping to find inspiration. What were the other items set to launch in that hour? Bottle warmer, white noise machine, tablet holder for the car— she knew the children's section of the channel's inventory like the back of her hand. Maybe there was something else out there she hadn't considered.

Maybe cleaning? Cleaning was a part of holiday travel, at least as she'd remembered it. There was always cleaning to do when guests were coming. Okay, check the cleaning section. She took a break to answer the emails that were piling up. She was going to fix it, Amy reassured her coworkers.

She navigated to a different section of the website. Here we are, she said to herself: cleaning and household inventory. Programmable washing machine, no, magic cleaning paste, no, foot mops—what on earth are foot mops? That sounds ridiculous. Amy clicked and investigated. She smiled to herself. This could work, actually! They had eight more hours until the show aired—plenty of time to adapt, and boy, were there a lot of foot mops in inventory. This could be heroic if she could unload some of them.

Amy couldn't wait to stay up and see how it went. It still pleased her immensely to put something new and strange on the air and then hear the excitement people felt when they found something that was perfect for them and their families. They even called in to the channel with testimonials.

There was an email from Conrad, as well. Apparently they had asked *him* to co-host the overnight show alongside his new girlfriend, Wendy. She had nothing against Wendy, just her own sadness at feeling left behind while others were building and growing lives. It was still odd to think of Conrad hosting a show about children and families. Well, maybe he just wanted the time with Wendy. They did make a cute couple, like Ken and Barbie.

The alarm on her phone went off—5:30 already? Time to work on dinner.

Luckily it was an easy recipe—chicken thighs, well-seasoned, roasted on high heat atop a bed of new potatoes and broccoli. One of Amy's weeknight favorites, and a treat to make for her mother—with enough for leftovers.

Amy added the pan to the oven and poured herself a glass of wine. As if on cue, she saw her view change to a wintry sunset of deep blues and magentas, magnified by the clear lake on the horizon. Now she knew what she could text the handsome photographer.

"Make sure you get a photo of tonight's sunset!" she sent.

"Done!" came the reply. Vincent texted a breathtaking photo, taken from the porch of the home he was shooting. She could see why people hired him. It looked like it was taken in paradise.

"Wow, that's gorgeous!"

He replied with a semicolon and a parenthesis. In other words, a wink. "Takes one to know one."

Oh dear, oh dear. The flirting. She was definitely not good at this. "Awwww" plus a smiley face was the most she could muster.

"What are you doing for dinner tonight?"

"Just making some chicken for my mom. You?"

"No idea—I was hoping I could convince you to show me around, but it looks like you're busy."

"Why don't you join us?" she typed, then debated hitting send, then realized she must look like she was typing a very long message, then wondered if she should change it and then—closing her eyes—hit send. She didn't want him to be looking at those three little dots that meant someone was taking a long time to send a message.

"I'd love to if it's no trouble—maybe I can pick your brain for some more local recommendations."

She sent Vincent her address and texted her mom the news that they were having a guest. The phone rang. Mom.

"Honey! I don't think I can make it tonight, these kittens are just too needy!"

"Mom, that never stopped you before."

"Well, uhhh—"

"Now I'll be alone with him and it'll be awkward."

"Oh please, you'll be fine. Have a wonderful night, dear! I hope it goes well."

"Ughhhh, okay. Thanks, Mom."

"And no feeding the cat people food!" Her mother laughed as she hung up the phone.

This was a date now, wasn't it? Her mom had played her and set her up!

Larry rolled over onto his back for tummy scratches. "Oh great, now you're all needy, too, you silly floof."

"Brrrrr," he purred.

It couldn't be a date, Amy decided. She knew nothing about this man, and for all she knew, he could have a girlfriend. It was just dinner. Even so, wearing a little makeup wouldn't hurt.

CHAPTER 4

"You didn't tell me I had to climb down a mountain of rickety stairs to get here. I almost turned around!"

Amy laughed. "Sorry about that. My grandfather built quite a staircase to get down here to this view."

Vincent looked around at the dark night. "I don't believe you. What view?" There was a mischievous twinkle to his smile. She laughed.

"I told you about the sunset, remember? Here, come on in, and meet Larry."

Vincent looked confused. "Larry's your-- who?"

"Cat. He's large and orange, and definitely in charge. Do you like cats?"

"A little—I haven't been around pets much. My mother was allergic, so we never had any growing up." Amy held up Larry for pets and Vincent reached out to him. "Wow, that's a big fluffy one, isn't it?"

Larry sniffed at Vincent's finger, confirming that he was a friendly presence, before consenting to be petted.

"I found Larry by the recycling bin at work. He's been my best buddy ever since."

"He looks like a good listener. Maybe I'll tell him some secrets later."

"Would you like some wine? I just opened a bottle."

"Sure, a little wine sounds nice."   Larry rolled onto his back, offering his belly. This cat was easy to please.

This feels easy for me, too, Amy thought to herself. Maybe I can do this. He seems to like me, and I like talking to him. I know I'm kind of an introvert who spends a lot of time on her laptop, but I feel calm around this man.

It seemed so simple now that they were chatting easily, but why did it feel so difficult sometimes? She handed Vincent a glass of wine. "So, what's your story? How did you become interested in photography?"

They took a seat at the table by the window, lit softly by the converted gaslamp that shone against the darkness of the lake. Vincent was taken in by Amy's eyes, framed by thick, natural lashes, and the flush of red she had painted on her lips. He realized how much he was looking at her, and looked away.

Now to answer the question she had asked. "Basically, I was a nerdy art kid. I know it doesn't look that way now." He was right. If anything, Vincent looked like an outdoorsman with good fashion sense. Like the tall, fortyish CEO of a company on holiday at his ski chalet. Amy didn't think he was her type, but she appreciated the efforts Vincent made to look handsome. "

I thought I could paint, or draw, or even sculpt, but when I took a photography class in high school, I found what I wanted to do." He sipped his wine. "There's something about photography being an art and a science at the same time. The technology keeps giving me new skills and options, but the core skills are consistent."

"Did you go to art school?" Gosh, this really was good wine, Amy thought. Better not have too much of it.

"Just went to state school, majored in business, like a lot of people do. But I took as many electives in art as I could. I worked at a real estate office after graduation, and somehow built what I have now." Amy guessed it wasn't that easy, that this man had worked hard, and tried to make others happy for a long time. Even now, it seemed like a job founded on delivering a high level of service to exacting clients.

"That's inspiring, honestly. I just started in one place, and I kind of…stayed and stayed. I'm still there."

"Sometimes I long for something like that. It's hard to live with this uncertainty. Not good for relationships either." Vincent avoided her gaze, while Amy tried to read his expression, unsure whether she should ask more.

She went for a middle ground. "Relationships can be challenging no matter what your job is."

"Cheers to that." They clinked glasses. This was fun, no expectations, and some time to get to know a lovely almost-stranger. Lyra had made Amy promise she would text at exactly ten o'clock that she was still alive, just in case Vincent had turned out to be a wolf in sheep's clothing. He wasn't that, but she was delighted to discover that he was no sheep either.

Just then, Amy felt a familiar touch on her leg. Larry. "What's up with you, Mr. Cat?"

"Is Larry okay with me being here? I do want to impress him." Vincent smiled.

She scritched Larry's ears, letting him nuzzle her and meow for a bit. He backed down and then walked around the braided rag rug, tracing its perimeter. "I think he smells the chicken cooking and wants some for a treat."

"I understand, Larry, I'm pretty excited myself." Larry looked at Vincent blankly, his mind set on chicken more than on this new human.

"Why don't I top up our glasses and get the salad together while I check on dinner?"

"Wonderful—how can I help?"

"I'm sure I can think of something for you to do." This is flirting—right? Oh I'm out of my depth, Amy thought. It seems to be working though, and she admitted she was a bit weak-kneed at the sight of Vincent, standing up to his full height in his cashmere sweater and jeans, following her into the kitchen.

As it turned out, Vincent was very helpful indeed. In the tight galley kitchen, he managed to make his way around, helping Amy wash and chop tomatoes and cucumbers for the salad while she made a vinaigrette. He brushed her arm just once as they shared the space, and let his hand linger there, before reaching across Amy for the salt, which he sprinkled on a slice of cucumber. As he popped it in his mouth, she teased, "save some appetite, sir."

"Yes, ma'am. More wine?" He set the glasses next to each other and she grabbed the bottle of red.

"Which is which?" Amy asked as he poured.

"I have a little trick I learned. I place glasses in alphabetical order from left to right. So Amy on the left, Vincent on the right. If Larry drank wine we could put him in the middle."

"Don't give him any ideas!" She laughed. Larry looked up at them, annoyed that he was not being fed chicken in that moment, and grumbled before padding off to the living room.

*

The chicken was fantastic, Vincent thought. Crispy skin on the seasoned chicken thighs, roasted veggies and potatoes, and the crisp salad, combined with the well-chosen wine—everything was simple and yet so tasty. He didn't feel like he was imposing, and it all felt comfortable. He smiled when he saw Amy set aside an unseasoned thigh to cool and shred as treats for Larry. Vincent wished he knew more women like her—what a shame that she lived so far away. He knew he shouldn't make a move on someone who lived—five?—states away, but it would only be polite to return the gesture. And he just had to be near her some more.

"I wish I could cook better to repay you—I confess I'm more of a summer barbecue kind of man. Grilled chicken, fresh corn, tomato salad, cold beer. Not the best weather for it, is it?"

"Aw you don't need to do that—I'm having a great time, really."

"Well, I'd still like to take you out, if you would like that."

She could barely breathe. "Yes, yes I would like that."

He exhaled. "Great, that sounds—yes. Good, Good." Stop babbling, he said to himself. "What, um, plans do you have for the next couple of days?" Did she detect a little nervousness in that deep voice of his?

She shrugged. "I know my mom will need some help, and I'm working remotely—"

"I didn't ask you anything about your work—here I am going on about mine—"

"It's fine, I promise. It'll give us something to talk about." Amy realized she was smiling an awful lot tonight.

"Well, I promise you my complete attention, whenever, and wherever."

"Noted. Let's check in tomorrow when I've had a chance to catch up with my mom."

They stood up. It was that time. The goodnight kiss. Would it happen? Both of them were silent as they walked to the door, enjoying the tension between them, not making eye contact. Amy opened the door, looked up at Vincent's deep brown eyes, and he leaned in quickly, brushing her lips gently with his.

It was like a jolt. Before she could realize what was happening, he backed away almost as quickly, and they said goodnight.

"Oh right, these stairs. Ugh. Be happy you're worth the climb, Ms. Amy!" Vincent joked as he headed up the steep flight to the main road. She laughed, closing the door.

Amy caught a glimpse of her reflection in the hallway mirror. She was flushed, smiling widely, and couldn't remember feeling this attractive in a long time. She knew she was in for something with this man, but had no idea what lay ahead.

In front of her, on the ground, Larry rolled around, enticing her to play. How was it possible to go from being a lonely woman with a cat to feeling like such a *desired* woman…with a cat?

*

"You had a date! You had a date!" Lyra was ecstatic.

"It was honestly great. He's interesting and genuine and really, well, hot."

"You deserve all of this. Getting back out there is a big deal, Amy. Well done."

"You know, I don't know that much about him," Amy realized. "I don't know his relationship history, much about his family, it's kind of a blank."

"Did Larry approve?" Larry and Conrad hadn't gotten along well, so this was an issue.

"Larry was down for the cause, Lyra. Rolling around, showing his belly, all of it."

"Good cat. Well done, Larry!" Larry paused. He appeared to recognize the sound of his name through the phone.

"He appreciates that. So yeah, I'm alive, and kind of hopeful."

"I wanted to check in with you about Cabo, but are you focused on this guy? We don't *have* to go, you know."

Amy knew Lyra really wanted to go, and Mexico in December sounded excellent. Maybe old Amy would stay here and place all her bets on Vincent, but she was going to put herself first early in this relationship, until she knew that he was serious about her.

Conrad had walked all over her; she could see that now. She didn't want some jealous boyfriend who thought going to the beach with a girlfriend would be an issue. That was just too controlling. So even though part of her brain was picturing a life of cozy snuggles with Vincent and Larry, looking out at the lake, enjoying a warm fire on a cool day, she had to take things one step at a time. Lyra would always be here for her, and they were going to have fun.

"I'm going! It's time to do things I like to do. Do you have any dates in mind?"

"What about the 27th through the 30th? That way you wouldn't have to travel on a holiday, and we'd get time with our families."

"Excellent! I never do anything on those days anyway."

"Me too. I just eat all the leftover cookies and binge Netflix." Amy could confirm this because she and Lyra had spent more than one holiday doing exactly that.

"What budget are we thinking here?" Both women were practical but also wanted to treat themselves. They settled on an all-inclusive resort on the beach in Cabo San Lucas, somewhere in the middle of the posted prices. "Great. I'll fly out of Richmond and change planes in Atlanta."

"This is going to be so much fun," Lyra enthused. "Leave it all to me—you can cash app me your portion whenever. You just focus on this rebound guy, and make him jealous by jetting off to Mexico." Would these choices make her seem more desirable, or just flakey? Amy had no idea. She just knew it would make her heart happy.

Maybe it would make her seem cool?

Lyra changed the subject. "Hey, what is everything like with Conrad? Do you have to see him at work?"

"Oh no, you just reminded me." Amy groaned. "He's on tonight and I need to watch him."

"Whatcha selling?" Lyra sometimes bought an item or two during Amy's overnight programming to support her.

"Foot mops." The words sounded so silly in her mouth.

"LOL. What now?"

"Yep. We have stock to clear out and I had an idea, so…we'll see how it goes, I guess."

"Okay, I don't know how late I'll be up. I have some grades to finish before break, but let me know how Conrad and his foot mops go."

Amy laughed. Lyra had a way with words. "See you soon!"

They hung up. This was a surprisingly lively night for her quiet lakeside retreat. First the unexpected date with Vincent, then travel plans to look forward to, and now, the thing Amy was avoiding. Conrad and Wendy live on the air, selling the foot mops Amy proposed. She hoped she was right about their sales potential. Only one way to find out.

*

The midnight hour programming on the shopping channel included two things: first, there was a special sale item that was being introduced that day. Those were planned far in advance, and Amy wasn't in charge of that selection process. But there was also programming that followed, and she had to find a place to show profits during later and later hours.

Amy didn't usually stay up to watch all of her programming—she would watch the first hour, cuddled up with Larry, and then make sure her phone was on in case of catastrophe. Working from home meant she didn't have to be up too early, except for the occasional meeting. Thankfully there was a large team working around the clock, and things tended to go well.

Even though they weren't at home in their usual snuggle spot, Larry knew it was TV time. They curled up on the sofa in front of the old, heavy television that overloaded a wheeled metal TV stand, and watched Wendy and Conrad introducing the daily deal—a vintage-style ceramic Christmas tree that would arrive just in time for the holiday. It was pretty cute, and would look nice in her apartment back home. Maybe she'd check and see if any were left when she arrived back home. It was pretty easy for staff to get hold of returned items after a holiday.

Amy sipped on her cup of chamomile tea, cozy with a purring Larry. She took deep breaths as her ex-boyfriend smiled lovingly at his new girlfriend. Perhaps they were right for each other. Perhaps her own right person would come soon, or was here. She let her mind wander back to the feeling of Vincent's lips on hers.

"You might wonder why a guy like me is staying overnight for the baby hour," Conrad said to the camera. "Well, we have some news for you." Wendy blushed as Conrad took her hand.

"We sure do!" Wendy smiled like the former beauty queen she was.

No, Amy thought to herself. This couldn't possibly be real. Some of the tea spilled out of her cup—her hands were shaking as she watched what looked like a glowing couple about to announce--

"This gorgeous, perfect woman and I are having our first child together in about six months—"

"This woman—I'm not just a woman! I'm your fiancée." Wendy beamed and held her left hand out to the camera. A camera zoomed in for a closeup on her engagement ring. Yikes, that was probably two carats.

Shocked, Amy sat staring, mesmerized by the sparkling diamond. She felt like this could not be her reality, but here it was. Would that have been

Amy's diamond if things had worked out with Conrad? Perhaps he had just been biding his time with her until someone had come along.

Two months ago, when they had broken up, Amy felt like her world was ending. She thought she had recovered tonight, laughing across from Vincent, enjoying the brush of his lips on her. Sure, he was handsome, ruggedly so, and kind, but the wounds from Conrad were so fresh.

Perhaps that was —wait, what did he say? Had Conrad said there were six months until he'd be a father?   That couldn't be. She must have misheard. Amy and Conrad were still together in October, though they hadn't been intimate for a few weeks by the time their relationship ended. She hadn't thought it was unusual, just that they were working things out.   Before she could fully understand what was happening, her attention was pulled back in by the television. There they were.

The foot mops.

She fixed her gaze on the TV and shifted into work mode. It was time to see whether her gamble would pay off.

"Our next product might not seem like it works for children, but it's actually a fun activity the family can do together!" Conrad stretched two shoe covers, covered in bright pink microfiber mop material, over his shoes. "These are foot mops! And they are now buy one get one for 50% off!" He looked handsome, and ridiculous, as he skated across the studio floor.

Wendy laughed. "So we can have matching ones, Conrad, and dance around the kitchen?"

"No! You will sit down and enjoy an evening of leisure, while our little offspring and I skate around the floors, picking up all the dust, then throw these bad boys into the washing machine." Amy was pleased in spite of herself. She resented their happiness, and how public it was; she couldn't help it. But Conrad was working his magic to sell those foot mops. He saw what Amy saw. That these silly, stretchy shoe covers were easy for children to use, to make cleaning up fun. And they could give their parents joy while also teaching responsibility.

The sales ticker in the corner of the screen proclaimed Amy's good fortune: there had been *thousands* of these foot mops sold during the presentation alone. They were inexpensive, but the profit margins were large as well. They probably cost around fifty cents to manufacture.

Wendy continued her own pitch, "I have cousins we see every Christmas, and they often don't understand how to help their mother with the cleaning, but with these foot mops, they can help out while enjoying some silly sibling fun at the same time. Make sure you purchase yours while we still have this promotion running. That way, they will still arrive before Christmas." Wendy was good, she had to admit. Amy was half-ready to buy her own foot mops even though she had no need for them.

It was getting late, though. She hoped her inbox in the morning would contain a note of appreciation for saving the midnight show, but for now it was time to get some sleep. Part of Amy liked that Wendy and Conrad were so happy together, and part of her felt pangs of regret and even shame. Their friends and colleagues wouldn't know that Conrad had left her *for* Wendy, and had apparently seen Wendy behind Amy's back when things were rocky. They would only see that Conrad had left her for someone better. And they could watch Conrad and Wendy's relationship grow on television.

It was indeed exhausting to consider, especially after a long day. When she finally made it to bed, Amy snuggled down into her warm flannel sheets and focused on her senses. The smell of the fresh sheets, the sound of the wind in the trees, even the taste of her toothpaste. She felt the tension of her muscles and tried to relax them one by one. Larry settled onto her hip and began to purr, acting as a weighted blanket. Everything was peaceful again.

CHAPTER 5

"You need to take Midnight!"

Amy was confused. Did her mother mean the midnight slot of the shopping—oh, she meant a cat. Of course it was a cat. The black cat, mother of the current fosters, including that sweet little gray smudge Ash.

"Mom, I can't! I have Larry. You know how he is."

"Well, Larry will just have to cope. I need to keep Midnight at the cottage for a few days to help wean her babies. I've been separating them for a few hours at a time, but they meow endlessly!" It was true that kittens were hard to wean if their mother was very close by.

"I guess we can try. But just the one cat, and only for a few days. I can keep one of them in the guest room if need be."

After they hung up, Amy was still doubtful. How can this work? She looked over at Larry. "Can you be a good cat with a visiting lady cat?" Larry flopped onto the floor and rolled around, enticing Amy to touch his belly.

"Are you being a loving cat, or is this a trap?" Only one way to find out: she reached down to stroke the soft belly fur.

Bite, kick, kick! Larry was play-fighting. "Awww, you tricked me again with the belly trap!" Larry rolled over onto his feet and ran off, in search of no one knew what.

The show last night had been a resounding hit—largely because of Conrad and Wendy's romantic announcement, but also because Conrad was simply adorable at selling foot mops. Amy had to admit that he looked like the kind of husband who wanted to give you a neck rub when you came home from work, and who always knew when it was time to punt and order takeout. A "wife guy." He hadn't been like that at all when they were together. In a way, that realization made it easier to move on. Although Amy was still seething at the knowledge that Conrad had had a foot (and apparently more) out the door at the end of their relationship, he and Wendy, she had to admit, seemed happy together. Besides, it was easier to forgive them after her date last night.

Vincent was looking like a step up, after all, in terms of compatibility. She remembered that kiss last night. It was so brief, yet it held the promise of more. Mmm, maybe there would be a longer session tonight. She luxuriated in fantasizing about their dinner date for just a minute.

*

"Here we are!" Mom entered, holding a tote in one hand and a cat carrier in the other.

Inside was a very quiet, fluffy black cat with large green eyes. She sniffed the air nervously, and looked around her through the carrier door. This was Midnight.

"Hello little mama," Amy greeted the cat in a soothing voice. "you're going to be just fine staying here with us."

"Where would you like me to put her?"

"Let's put her in the guest room for the first night at least. Larry hasn't been there and I can close the door."

They set up Midnight in the guest room, with a spare litter tray, food, and water, then opened the carrier door. She poked her furry head out hesitantly.

Just then, Larry stuck his paw under the door and yowled.

Midnight dashed out of her carrier and ran under the bed.

"Larry, mind your manners!"

Larry hissed from the other side. Oh boy, this was going to be trouble.

"They'll be fine," Rebecca said. "I've had plenty of rescues and it's usually like this. Midnight will settle in just fine. Probably bring her back into town tomorrow for a few hours just in case she's still producing milk, keep her comfortable as she weans."

Amy bent down to peek under the bed to where Midnight lay. She saw only a pair of glowing green eyes. The eyes blinked. "I'll check on you later, little mama."

Amy and her mother came out to give Larry his desired attention, but not until his inquisitive nose had pestered their hands and feet, seeking this new cat scent that had entered the house. He stalked off in a huff to the other bedroom.

"It's fine, Amy. I promise they'll get used to each other. Change will be good for Larry."

"Well, I'm trying to be comfortable with a new outlook on life myself, so maybe Larry and I can learn together."

They sat quietly together, taking in the lake view. Although it was chilly outside, the sun was out and its rays danced over the rippling water. Amy didn't know what it was about this view, from a comfortable chair, drinking coffee, but it was truly the best thing in the world. She never wanted to leave.

"The stress is just melting away, huh, Mom? Don't you miss it here?"

"Sometimes. But those stairs to this cottage? Just no. Your dad used to call them third cup of coffee stairs, because you'd keep drinking coffee at the table to avoid climbing them." Rebecca laughed.

"So what's the plan for today?" Amy asked.

Her mother shrugged. "Let's take it easy today after yesterday. Besides, I *do* want a third cup of coffee while I avoid the stairs and hear about your date."

"Coming right up. You'll be happy to know that I'm checking in with him today about going out again."

Rebecca clapped her hands together. "Oh good! It was just as I hoped. Me staying away meant that you two could get to know each other. I just want you to be happy, hon."

Amy let her eyes wander as she and her mother gossiped. The small patch of grass behind the cottage had seen better days. Both sides of the yard had brick walls, keeping their view private and providing a buffer for sound.

Her grandfather had worked as a contractor and one long holiday weekend he and a couple of friends used leftover supplies and a few cold beers to build these walls. The walls were in sore need of a pressure wash and repair, and the brick grill the men had added to the corner of the yard on a whim was covered in dirt and twigs. She wondered whether it even worked, all these years later.

Her mother noticed Amy's silence and followed her gaze. She sighed. "I keep meaning to clean up back there but I have no energy to do it, Amy. Do you think we could find some high school kid home on break who wants some money to clean it out?"

Amy felt sad that she had reminded her mother of the ever-mounting to-do list that occupied her life since they'd lost her father. "I was thinking about doing it myself, actually. I'd like a little distraction and it would be, I don't know, *meaningful* to me."

"By all means!" Rebecca said. "You know where the supplies are." She sighed. "I miss the bright red dock. You can't even see the paint anymore. It looked so cheerful with your grandmother's—"

"Geraniums! Yes, I was thinking of her. I miss her." Even as her grandmother lay sick in a nursing home at the end of her life, she loved to talk about the blooming trees and the birds who came to visit her. She had always taken joy in the small things. It was one of the personality traits Amy hoped to emulate.

"I do, too, honey. I miss when we were a big group, all together, with your grandpa grilling steaks, insisting you get your very own steak even though you were such a small thing." Those had been wonderful times, and now the women were looking at the ghosts of those happy moments.

After her mother had left, Amy sat with her thoughts for a time. Coming home wasn't what she had expected. There was the pleasure of being away, certainly, and the nostalgia she felt being home. But nostalgia had a component of sadness to it as well, and there were memories of the absence of love here, too. Many of those she had loved, who had loved her, were no longer here to comfort Amy when she was upset.

The memories and the time she had with her grandparents here were real, though, and she pulled these memories around her as she sat remembering the happy times they had shared. She said a quick prayer for her family, and for all who were lonely at Christmas, and decided it was time to get to work.

*

She had spent nearly two hours of clearing out muck and twigs before Amy checked her phone and saw three messages from Vincent. Well, that felt good. She'd be sore tomorrow from the work outside but she'd see him later tonight, and working with her hands had been just what she needed.

They were going to the Emporium, a former general store that passed for fine dining in town. It was a date night restaurant, and she had a handsome and fun date to take her out. If the Emporium was a little bit stuck in the 1990s, who was she to judge? Amy opted not to look in the mirror before washing up in the kitchen sink because she had a feeling that there was a big goofy grin on her face.

Whatever expression she wore turned to concern when she heard the yowling in the next room.

Larry was in a panic. He ran to Amy, yowled, then ran to the bedroom door where Midnight lay and yowled again. "I know, buddy," she soothed. "She's not here for long. It's okay." Another yowl. But this one not from Larry.

Amy looked at the door more closely and, in the shadows, saw a paw dart out and swipe around, searching for something. "Aww, hey there, kitty. You upset in there?"

Larry walked to the door and sniffed the paw. He made a soft grumbling noise.

Then he nuzzled the paw against his face. Midnight withdrew her paw. He looked up at Amy.

"Larry! You kissed her hand, you Romeo." He circled Amy, seemingly unsure.

Midnight was quiet. Perhaps she was sniffing her paw to learn more about her new housemate.

The cat then made a cheerful peeping sound from behind the door. Larry chirped in response.

Should I open the door? Amy wondered. It hadn't been very long but the cats seemed to want to meet.

She opened the door. Each cat looked shocked. Midnight was surprisingly brave. She put one paw in front of the other, stepping cautiously across the threshold. Larry looked worried and hissed quietly, but she ignored him. He looked around in Midnight's room to see whether there were other cats inside. Satisfied, he returned. The two sat at opposite ends of the braided rug and appeared to be taking one another in. Perhaps this was the next step after the initial awareness of a fellow feline, just sitting in space together and learning to cohabit.

Amy sat in complete stillness, hoping that her quiet would inspire theirs. This was successful for the first minute or two. But as with most quiet, it made her aware of her body and its needs in that moment: she was hungry from yard work, hadn't showered, and she needed a bathroom break. Ugh.

Okay, tiptoe to the bathroom, no sudden movements. When she finished, Amy craned her neck around the edge of the door. Still no movement from the cats.

She took a quick shower and returned. Still no movement.

She walked past the cats on the rug, hoping to sneak to the kitchen for a sandwich.

Each looked up at her peacefully. Midnight blinked her eyes from behind an elegant black cloud of fur. Was it this easy for them to live together? Had Larry actually been lonely and in need of a cat friend?

Food first. As she had anticipated, both cats followed her to the kitchen. Amy's turkey sandwich became a source of great feline consternation, and both cats were duly fed small pieces, first rinsed of salt and seasoning. Amy herself feasted on turkey, sourdough, lettuce, tomato and cream cheese—her favorite. All three residents of the cottage were fed and happy at last.

*

A few work emails later, and Amy was feeling pretty satisfied with how things were going. The foot mops were still selling well—the channel's website had showed a clip of Conrad skating around in them and people thought it would make a fun novelty gift. Tonight they would air the very last show that featured shipping guaranteed before Christmas, and her "Christmas in a Box" last-minute décor show was a tried-and-true success. There would be some backlog when she came back to Florida, certainly, but she had worked late into the night for weeks preparing for the holiday season. Now, other than the occasional setback, she was mostly just monitoring her work for emergencies.

She wrote a few notes on her pad. Things to do before Christmas, presents for her mother and the cats, stocking stuffers, maybe something for Vincent if that wasn't too weird an idea. It must be too soon, but maybe a plant from the nursery would be all right.

The phone rang. Vincent.

"Hey there, can't wait to see—"

"Amy. I'm glad I caught you in time." He sounded rushed.

"What's wrong—everything okay?"

"Um, actually something's come up. I'll have to cancel taking you out tonight. Sorry for the late notice."

Her heart sank. She was dying to know every detail but she knew she couldn't grill Vincent like that. Not after one dinner together. After they hung up, Amy called her mother and invited her to the Emporium for dinner instead. Her mother deserved the treat, and they had missed out on the time together yesterday.

*

Later that evening, Rebecca and Amy were waiting at the restaurant's bar to be seated, chatting about a summer vacation from two decades ago, one that Amy had barely remembered. The family had vacationed at a summer rental in Maine, on a remote, rocky beach. It had sounded wonderful in theory, but the water was cold, the rocks were sharp, and foot-protecting water shoes were an invention that had yet to reach the Guillaume family. It had also rained nearly every day.

"I honestly remember the rain as the best part of it," Amy reminisced, thinking of time spent with her parents on the screen porch, playing cards through a downpour by the light of a kerosene camping lamp. "When was the last time we went together as a family?"

"Oh! I remember that one. You were a freshman in college. I could tell you were done with the 'wholesome family vacation' part of life and wanted to party with your friends instead." Rebecca looked sad. It was hard for Amy to see her mother as someone who was worried about losing her when she grew up.

"I'm sorry, Mom. I wish we could go back and have more of those days together. I realize now how limited the time actually was."

Rebecca shook her head. "No, that's how things are supposed to be. Raising children turns into raising adults. I felt lucky for the years we did have with just the three of us, Amy. No regrets over here."

"But aren't you lonely?"

"That isn't the same question, though. Sure, I get lonely when I'm not busy, but I keep busy and I have so many wonderful memories. I'd still like us to take a trip together sometime if you'd like, though, hon."

Amy was about to answer in the affirmative when she remembered: her Mexico trip with Lyra. Her mother must have seen Amy's expression change.

"It's okay, Amy. We don't have to if you're too busy."

"No! It isn't that. I'd love to, Mom. We should plan something special together. I just remembered that I'll be out of town for a few days after Christmas and forgot to tell you. I think it's the 27th through midday on the 30tht."

Her mother smiled. "Oh, sure. It's not with Vincent, is it?" That did seem a little too soon.

"No—Lyra wanted to go on a girls' trip to Mexico and we decided to go together while school is out of session. Do you think you could mind the cats for me while we are gone?"

"Oh, of course. Happy to help. You know, it never ceases to amaze me that Lyra teaches calculus. I know I shouldn't judge, but if we were to make a list of women in six-inch heels and women who also teach calculus, it would be a very short list."

Amy laughed. "And she'd be at the top."

Her mother smiled.

"Excuse me, ladies, I have your table ready—" They turned to look at the server approaching the bar.

As the server led them to the table, Amy stood up straight, a shiver sent down her spine. Vincent, it turned out, *was* at the Emporium for dinner tonight, but not with her.

Vincent sat there, directly in front of the bay window, leaning in to whisper in the ear of a beautiful young woman who was drinking a glass of champagne.

Amy grabbed her mother's arm. "Let's get out of here." She gestured to Vincent while she looked for the exit, her heart racing.

Vincent and Rebecca's eyes met, the shock registering on his face. But before he could respond, the two women had vanished.

CHAPTER 6

Amy couldn't take in enough of the crisp evening air when she and her mother turned right on the sidewalk in front of the Emporium.

She felt like she was taking the deepest breaths imaginable. She felt panicked, yet simultaneously embarrassed that she was panicked. They had only been on one date, after all.

Who was Vincent with at that table for two? What if he had a girlfriend and had lied?

What if he was married?

It could be innocuous, sure. Why wouldn't he have told her, though, if it were an innocuous meeting? If her cousin had come into town, or a colleague, Amy would have mentioned it to Vincent when postponing plans.

"Amy, slow down," her mother called from a few steps back. She stopped.

"I'm sorry, Mom. I don't know what to do. I can't think."

"Honey, I know. Here, let's go to the diner and get some food in you, okay?"

Amy nodded. The women walked on in silence as they made their way a few blocks south to the diner.

Outside, the air in Haverton was crisp and wintry, but still a little damp. There were still wet autumn leaves on the sidewalks even though the Christmas decorations were gaily lit and festooning the shops of the town. Most of the shops were no longer open these days. Sometimes someone from Richmond would move in and open a cheese shop or a café for a few years. Infrequently, they would stick around, but more often than not, they would close after a few years. The town had enough money to support a few businesses, certainly, but the competition from online shopping and large chain stores had made it harder for the "little guys" to succeed.

The diner was an exception. It had been there forever. It didn't even have a sign anymore. The diner was just known to the town, was open all day, and attracted everyone from families, to the high school drama club, to senior citizens.

The women sat down and ordered decaf coffee and pancakes. It was time for comfort food and a hot drink, but not one to keep Amy up all night. She didn't want to be awake at all right now.

"I really don't know what to think, Mom. I feel ashamed for being hopeful, but beyond that I don't know."

"It didn't look good, Amy. Still, there might be a reasonable explanation."

Amy thought about this possibility. "Even if it's not, we don't live in the same area anyway, though. It might have been a fun flirtation, but he is never moving to Miami to be with me or anything, and I really don't know him at all." She was trying to talk herself out of caring.

"That's true. And as you said, you don't know him. It's a shame though. If he's serious about that girl, he shouldn't have gone out with you, and vice-versa."

Her mother was right. Amy added extra butter and syrup to her pancakes. Today was not a day for dieting.

"Pancakes are like having dessert for a meal, aren't they?" she said, reaching for a drink in between bites.

"You know, Amy, that fancy food they have at the Emporium wouldn't be as good as this, and this is a third of the price."

"True that, Mom. I'm much happier. Let's figure out our Christmas plans, then."

It was already the 18th, and the holiday was a week away. There would be a day for cookie-baking, a day for tree-trimming (while eating the cookies), a day for charity, a day for binging movies, a night for church, a night for looking at Christmas lights—they were running out of days and nights and the presents still hadn't been wrapped. What a week it was going to be! The kittens were weaning and the cats were getting on reasonably well. Amy even had a surprise or two planned for her and her mother.

And there was no time for getting hung up on a man.

When the mother and daughter emerged into the chilly December night, both felt connected and energized for the week ahead. It had been a good night after all, in spite of the shock. Family was always the right choice.

*

Amy used the flashlight app on her phone to descend the steep stairs home, then pocketed her phone once she was under the halo of the porch light. She had forgotten to worry about the cats, but those feelings all resurfaced at once when she entered the cottage.

She turned on the light and prepared for the worst.

The cats were now cuddled on the braided rug, fast asleep. Larry raised a sleepy head to look at Amy, then settled back down to sleep.

Her heart melted. There was a love story happening in her house in spite of her own messy love life. Two lonely cats snoozing together, staying warm, feeling connected in a way only they understood. She felt a twinge of guilt for having deprived Larry of a companion for so long. He needed another cat to love, and she'd talk to her mom about making a home for Midnight tomorrow.

Amy had turned off notifications on her phone before dinner and dreaded checking messages. She didn't want to see Vincent's excuse, or some half-baked apology come up on her screen. She had been wrong about him, that's all. He was tall and charming and fun to be with, but she didn't know that much about him, truth be told.

Instead, she grabbed her laptop and curled up on the sofa. Her water bottle was right next to her where she'd left it and she took a swig. It was time to plan those Christmas surprises.

Since her grandparents had died, there hadn't been an effort to decorate the lake cottage for Christmas. It looked cozy, sure—the wood, the fireplace, and the view took care of that—but the twinkle of fairy lights and the holiday spirit were notably absent.

She booted up her laptop and smiled. Because Amy had access to her workplace's warehouse site, she was able to request direct orders from purchasing. Time to place a last-minute order just in time for Christmas.

She found an old-fashioned ceramic Christmas tree that was the perfect size for the cottage, some cheerful blue snowflake mugs for tea and cocoa by the fire, cozy socks and treats for Amy and her mother, and even some silly presents for the cats. Amy was responsible with her money, but a little retail therapy now and then—with her employee discount—was pretty harmless.

Everything would be delivered to the cottage by the twenty-third. Perfect.

Now for what she'd been avoiding: her phone. It sat next to her like a menacing brick.

There was just one message. A text from Vincent. "Call me when you get this."

The message had been sent an hour after the restaurant incident, and it was now past midnight. Too late to call, especially when he might be on a date or fast asleep.

Amy knew it was smartest to wait to send her reply, perhaps until morning when she felt calmer, even though her feelings were pulling her toward making that call. Bedtime it would be. There was too much going on and she needed a little time to process.

Larry and Midnight were still in the living room. She hoped they would join her in a cuddle, because this was a lonely night for her.

It took a long time to fall asleep. Amy tried to soothe herself with thoughts of Christmas and of traveling to Mexico. She nearly drifted off, imagining even more time by the lake this summer, when Miami would be too hot to bear.

And then the phone screen lit up on the nightstand next to her. Oh no.

Vincent again.

"Never mind. Thanks again for dinner. Merry Christmas and good luck with everything. Vincent."

Her eyes flew open in shock. She read the two texts a dozen times. In waiting to reply, had Amy just been dumped? And by a man who was taking out another woman?

And that was how Amy Guillaume found herself alone and wide awake at two o'clock in the morning, a week before Christmas.

CHAPTER 7

The next few days offered Amy cozy and charming distractions from Vincent. There was nothing like the pure pleasure of Christmas at home, surrounded by old memories, and making new ones with Mom.

They had spent a full day on baking: cutout cookies, chocolate crinkles, and the special cherry walnut cookies Amy's father had loved. Even though he wasn't there, it wouldn't be Christmas without his favorite cookies.

Amy knew her mother's hope for the holiday, though Rebecca had never said it directly. Her mother hoped that, by now, there would be a son-in-law to help eat the cookies and trim the tree—maybe even a toddling grandchild to spoil.

Still, the living room tree looked beautiful in the corner by the fireplace. The small room was fragrant with evergreen scent, and the additional tree branches they had found at the garden center festooned the mantle, setting off red pillar candles in the old ceramic reindeer candleholders that had belonged to Rebecca's mother.

They had decorated the tree yesterday, placing their favorite ornaments front-and-center. The macaroni star, spray-painted gold, from Amy's preschool days, the antique miniature brass horns that had come from England with their great-grandmother. The photos of their little family as it grew.

There were ornaments to be hung up on the back of the tree—also a tradition. Amy's father had hated an old 1980s photo of him with a giant mustache and always placed that ornament out of reach. It had become a family joke. As had the giant pink sequin ornament one of Amy's boyfriends had given her as a Christmas gift one year. That relationship did not survive, but they had to laugh at the silly, huge ornament when they unpacked it every year.

Amy had responded to Vincent's goodbye text the following morning with a polite "Merry Christmas!" He had probably gotten back together with a girlfriend or something. Amy had seen a missed call from Vincent only once since their text exchange, and had had the strength not to take it. He was allowed to move on with his life, and she wished him well. She didn't need to hear excuses or have an awkward conversation about why he liked that other woman better. The holidays were hard enough without piling on rejection.

There was Christmas ahead, and Cabo, and she was feeling more confident, just as she'd hoped. Now it was the twenty-second of December, and work had nearly slowed to a halt. Free shipping promotions had ended, and the only sales airing had been planned months ago.

Amy sipped from her water bottle as she sent off some emails and set up her autoreply. She was only checking messages occasionally until January 1st, and could not wait to let go of work obligations. Even when this job was good, it was still challenging.

As her last work-related email before the holidays, Amy decided to do the right thing by Conrad. "Hey there! I heard you and Wendy are expecting—congrats! Have a great holiday. –A".

Satisfied, she returned to her web browser to do the crossword puzzle. It was time to restart her streak.

*

Amy distracted herself with holiday excitement, looking at her favorite recipe blogs for Christmas breakfast and dinner ideas, and wrapping presents for her mother. She had made sure to go a little overboard on the stocking stuffers this year. Her mother had spent so long looking for just the right tiny things for Amy's stocking when she was little that it felt good to do the same in return.

She watched *It's a Wonderful Life* for a little while on the television while she wrapped the miniature stocking gifts in candy-striped paper. Her favorite film had become a Christmas movie because it was set at Christmastime, but it was really more of a love story than anything.

James Stewart and Donna Reed were humming "Buffalo Gals Won't You Come Home Tonight?" and strolling down the street, on the way to fall in love, and Amy wondered what it was she had missed in her own life.

She had had what they did, in more modern terms: there was a small town, friendly people, and handsome young men all around when she was growing up. How could someone cross that bridge, to move from merely existing in a space to drawing someone in, such that they fell in love with you? She could talk to men, attract them even, but after this long, it was hard not to take it personally when they didn't *feel* anything for her

What did Mary Hatch do to become Mary Bailey? Amy watched the film like a detective. Mary was in the right place at the right time. She had a vision of what she wanted, who she wanted, even where she wanted to live—the old house no one else wanted. Her hero was a man who thought he was a failure. Was imagination the key to love? George Bailey had offered to lasso the moon for her, but Mary embroidered it on a pillow to make it happen.

Instead of realizing that two movie characters might offer a key to finding love, Amy felt disappointed. The film made it seem harder than ever, as though love were an act of creation between two people who already wanted to be together. She worried that she didn't even have the first part: desire.

Amy turned off the television to take a moment for herself. You're supposed to like this movie, she told herself. Sigh.

Just then, Larry walked by to check on her.

"Still my guy, Larry? I know you and Midnight are besties, but I could use a cuddle, too." She scooped the sturdy orange cat into her arms and snuggled him. He began to relax and purr in her arms. What a sweetie he was.

Midnight sprawled out next to Amy's hip, joining in the comfort. Soon there were two purrs, and Amy let herself breathe evenly. She let her racing thoughts rest for a minute. This was real, too, and this was its own kind of love.

*

"Scratch! Scratch! Scratch!" The cats chased one another furiously on the wood floors, slipping as they tried—unsuccessfully—to slow down and change directions.

"Is this your mad half-hour?" Amy asked the cats. Midnight stopped and stared Amy's way, wide-eyed and puffed up with excitement. She then resumed her chase of Larry. Larry seemed to be a little more coordinated these days from the exercise. The chasing and wrestling must be a good work out, she mused. She was lucky that the wide wooden plank floors had seen a lot of wear, and that a few cat scratches would barely register to the eye.

The next scratch Amy heard came from outside the house. She wondered whether her packages of Christmas goodies had arrived early and went to the door to investigate.

When she opened the door, Vincent stood on the porch, holding pine boughs and branches. He looked caught in the act. "Amy, hi. I didn't know if you were available—"

"I'm here." Her heart was beating out of her chest, it felt. She didn't know what to say, and wondered whether saying as little as possible would be the best choice. She must protect herself after the drama of the last week.

He smiled, nervously. "I'm on my way out of town, and wondered if you could use any of these to decorate. It would be a shame to get rid of them, but I can also put them in the garden waste bin if you've already decorated."

She looked at the branches, remembering her awkward run-in with Vincent at the garden center. It wasn't the branches' fault this had happened.

"Sure," she answered. "I was going to do some decorating today. Thank you."

Amy opened the door and Vincent entered. He set the foliage on the kitchen counter, where Amy could arrange it with the least amount of mess. "You know, Amy. I really did want to take you out."

"I appreciate that," she said, unable to meet his eye. "Obviously things are complicated for you."

"They aren't now. I've realized that."

Amy blushed in spite of herself. "It's really none of my business. I barely know you."

"And I'm sorry for that. Sometimes I'm a good talker and other times—well, I just don't know what to say."

"Anyway," she ventured, "you're leaving town now anyway, I take it?"

Vincent looked up to the road where his car was parked. "Uhhhh, there isn't anywhere to stay, unfortunately. The folks who hired me want people in for an open house now, so I'll have to head out."

Amy couldn't invite him to stay with her, though a part of her wanted to. What if there were something unsafe that she didn't know? Alone in the middle of winter with a strange man? With snow predicted, no less? There wasn't anyone handsome enough for that. But maybe they could mend things for a few more minutes. She would feel better with closure.

"Would you like a cup of tea? I was just about to make a pot."

He seemed relieved. "Yes, I'd like that. It's really kind of you."

She met his eye for a brief second and saw his eagerness to make amends. "Sure, no problem. And thanks again for bringing these by."

There was a thick silence between them as Amy fired up the kettle and prepared the teapot. The tea steeped.

"How long of a drive do you have?" Amy asked.

"It's up to me, I guess. Thank you—" he took a cup from Amy and held it out while she poured. "I have three hours until I'm at my place, but four hours until I reach my parents' house."

"That isn't too bad, then."

"No, not at all. My girlfriend—ex-girlfriend, I mean—lived in DC. That was about six hours, depending on traffic."

Amy blurted the words before she could think: "Was that her I saw you with?"

"Yes. We had already broken up, so you know. She—"

"You don't have to tell me," she interjected quickly. "I barely know you. It's really none of my business."

"The thing is, though," Vincent slowed down, taking a sip. "I don't mind it being your business. I enjoy being with you."

No! She hoped she wasn't going to fall for this, and here Amy found herself smiling anyway. "Well, thank you." Don't keep talking, Amy.

"I'm really sorry. Karrie drove out of her way to meet up with me for dinner, so I thought I would give it a try, and everything went wrong. Just—everything. She left right after dinner."

Amy struggled to contain her surprise. This was not what she had imagined. "Oh, I didn't know."

"I didn't know how to talk to you about it. Thanks for letting me tell you now, though." He smiled, more at ease.

"Would you like to sit down?" she offered.

They sat in the places where they had laughed over dinner a few days before. "It really is beautiful here during the day." Vincent admired the yard and the view, "it must look incredible when the sun is out and everything is in bloom. I'd love to see it."

"The birds are one of my favorite parts of summer here," Amy added. "There are so many kinds, songbirds, too. Though you wouldn't believe it on a moody day like this."

"I like moody. You know, I think my only time in Virginia in summer, I was six and we went to Colonial Williamsburg. I was more interested in the horses and sheep there."

Amy laughed, "We always went there for school trips. I loved the blacksmith's shop." She paused and reached out her hand to smooth out the edge of one of the placemats.

Vincent was looking at her, she knew. He placed his hand on the table across from hers. Then touched the back of her hand gently with his fingertips.

"Do you think I could take you out tonight instead?" Vincent asked. "There has to be a place I can grab a room in town somewhere. It doesn't feel right to leave like this."

He was stroking the back of her hand now. It felt good, gentle, comforting.

"Yes, I would like that. Yes." Amy could no longer think logically. She felt woozy and giddy all at once. This was what she had hoped for the other day, and she hadn't quite been able to bury it. Maybe she was a pushover, but she was learning to give love a chance, and this was a step.

Slowly, Amy rotated her palm upward and flexed her fingers. She closed her hand around his.

"Thanks for giving me another chance," he said softly.

"Thanks for trying again. Sometimes I need a little bit of a nudge."

They sat like that for a minute, happy in one another's company.

"Do you mind if I use your laptop to look for a room? Mine is up in the car."

"Oh, sure!" She helped him log in. "And thank you, sir. I appreciate the gentlemanly approach."

"You deserve it for putting up with me." He began to search.

"Why don't I call into town and find us a table while you look for a place to stay?"

"Sounds like a plan, and you know the best places anyway. Anywhere you like."

*

An hour later, following more tea and conversation, they were on the road in Vincent's SUV, their destination a little steakhouse tucked away behind an old hitching post on the way to town. It was rustic and romantic at the same time, and there was always a wood fire burning in the wintertime.

"Looks like snow tonight," the server said as she seated them. "Glad you're here before it hits."

"Indeed," Vincent agreed.

"I guess we can only linger a little bit, but I'm glad we are here."

"Me too," he replied, "and who knows? Maybe the storm will shift."

This wasn't the date Amy had expected, but that relaxed, easy feeling had returned. In spite of what had happened the other night, they still wanted to give this a try. She was happy he had come by the cottage. They ordered a bottle of red wine and settled into their comfy booth for two near the fireplace.

"Would you mind, just to get it out of the way, letting me know a little bit about what was going on the other day? I don't need to know it all, but it really was kind of hard to see." Amy held her breath, hoping she was expressing herself well.

"No, yeah, you're right. I should tell you. I mentioned Karrie, my ex-girlfriend. We broke up about six months ago and, well, she broke up with me. Because of the long distance thing. She had left me for someone who broke up with her about a month ago, and I think she got lonely and decided to come find me. Maybe it was the holidays, I don't know."

"I see. So she figured you would just be waiting for her?"

"I'm pretty sure that's what she thought. But she also expected me to be bending over backwards to win her back, even though she was the one who ended things. I was too hurt for that, and I wanted an apology from her. So after you left, things took a turn, and well, to make a long story short, I don't think I want to show my face in that Emporium place again."

She tried not to smile. "I'm sorry about all of that, but I promise you the Emporium has seen some messy behavior. I promise you they've forgotten."

"That's a relief." The server poured them their cabernet and set down fresh bread and butter.

"And you deserved an apology from Karrie, since she had treated you so poorly."

"Part of me wants to confide in you about this, and the other part of me is dying to know what else you've seen in the Emporium!"

This time Amy smiled and chuckled. "Suffice it to say that it was *the* restaurant to go before prom in high school, and there were so many couple arguments, *high-school couple* arguments. So much drama, I promise you that between your date last night and now, there's been a few drunk uncles, a breakup, a failed marriage proposal, really I promise you shouldn't worry."

He was smiling and laughing too. "What do you know about it? Maybe my drunk uncle came by and proposed to her?" He shrugged. "She might say yes, though. He's quite charming."

Now they were both laughing. Amy wiped a tear. "You're too much."

He raised his glass to her. "To second chances."

She clinked her glass against his. "Absolutely."

"We should probably order something, though. Don't want to keep the staff out in the snow."

"Yes, let's. Steaks are great here, if you're into that. They have good fish in the summer, but I don't know what the situation is in winter."

He perused the menu. "I think steak sounds perfect. Would you like to share some sides? Asparagus and maybe some potatoes?"

"I'd love to, on both counts. Potatoes au gratin?"

"That's the one."

They ordered and settled back, each taking in the other's face. Amy, lit by candlelight and the glow of the nearby fire, was all softness, and Vincent's handsomeness became more pronounced. She looked into his brown eyes, content.

He broke the silence.

"So I've been dying to hear more about you, and I don't think I can wait any longer. I'll have to invent things if you don't tell me—"

"I see, so I'd better cooperate, huh? Hmm, well, my ex-boyfriend was cheating on me with someone we work with, and now they're engaged and expecting a baby." She sat back in her chair and took a sip of wine.

He looked aghast.

She brushed her hand to the side as if to brush away the memory. "No, it's fine. Well, it isn't, but they seem better together than he and I were, so I can't be *that* upset."

"Still, though, that hurts a lot."

"You're right. It does. Being far away from it feels much better. And um, I'm enjoying this date very much, which makes forgetting much easier."

Vincent raised his glass to her. "I'm enjoying it, too."

When the food arrived, piping hot and well-seasoned, their conversation quieted. "I must be hungry, because I'm not able to talk," Amy remarked.

"Same here—you do you, pretty lady. Eat up." Vincent winked.

"I don't know what it is about eating food cooked over a wood fire in the dead of winter, but it always tastes wonderful."

"In college, we used to fire up the kettle grill to make hot dogs, even when it was cold outside. A charred hot dog and a beer in January is a pretty great combination. If you get the right chill in the air, it keeps your beer cold as you grill."

"Oh no, now I'm getting hungry for a hot dog and I'm in the middle of eating." Amy laughed, then stopped when she noticed something out of the corner of her eye.

Snow. And, come to think of it, night.

While they had been enjoying their meal, the sun had set and the promised storm had arrived. Fluffy snow floated down to the pavement outside. What a beautiful sight. Dangerous and beautiful.

"Boy, it's really coming down out there." Vincent shook his head, a bit chagrined.

"Yep. It's gorgeous. Not convenient, but gorgeous."

He smiled at Amy. "Awww, just like you."

"Ha! You have a corny side, I take it."

"Maybe."

"For real though," she was thinking out loud, "how are we both going to make it to our places?"

"Well," Vincent pondered. "You need to be the priority, not just to be gentlemanly, but also because you have a needy cat depending on you."

"*Two* needy cats, now, actually. But yes, you're right about that."

"Did a cat just wander in, or?" He looked amused by the twists and turns of her life.

"No, I took her in for my mom for a few days and, well, she's not going anywhere now. They call it a 'foster fail.' It's a happy failure. But how far away is the room your booked for tonight?"

He looked on his phone for the booking confirmation and showed it to her.

"Okay, that's half an hour in the opposite direction. Even my mom's house is too far out from that." Amy hemmed and hawed. She wanted to invite Vincent to stay, and she knew in her heart that he'd spend another couple of hours at the cottage flirting and talking—and maybe a little more?—if they went back home after dinner on a clear night.

"I'll take you home and then, worst comes to worst, I'll have a little rest in the car if I can't make it to the hotel. I've done it before and it's—"

"You are *not* doing that. Just—no. You'll be killed by a snowplow or freeze to death or." She lost her train of thought, then recentered. "So. We have two bedrooms in the house. As a new friend, of course you can stay in the guest room. I have two very fierce guard cats to protect me if you get any ideas."

"Understood. You might be my most attractive friend, though. I'll have to go through some pictures when we get back to your—"

"Okay, stop that before I change my mind." The flirting really was too delicious to stop, and he was so *funny*. She had forgotten how to flirt, or so she'd thought, and just a few days ago she'd never picture herself enjoying a man's company this much. It was fun, all of the banter.

The server brought the bill early so that they could settle up and head out. It was still a lovely meal, the quiet of the snow making the nearly-empty restaurant seem more intimate. Even the old drafty windows added to the romance, causing Amy to burrow into her sweater a bit, warmed by the flirtation and the wine.

They stepped out into the crisp air, gentle snow falling silently around them, the car covered in downy piles of it.

Vincent leaned over, swiftly, and drew Amy in to his chest. Before she could react, he leaned down and kissed her, all warmth in the middle of the chill. He took her head in both hands and deepened his kiss as she reflexively moved in closer. She lay a hand on his strong chest, letting him warm her, wanting to be seduced.

They pulled away and looked at one another, speechless. She leaned back in and gave him a tiny kiss on his mouth. "Thank you for keeping me warm."

Vincent drew her close to him again. "Thank *you*. I don't think I can stop kissing you, but we should probably try." He leaned in once more, and kissed her gently. Amy stroked his arm, noticing the strength of his biceps.

"Mmm, you feel good."

"You too." He opened her snow-covered car door and ushered her in. "I'll start this up for you and clear off the snow so we can get you home."

Amy must have floated into the seat, for she didn't remember how she got in, how they got home, anything other than the tremendous pull of these new feelings. Vincent had this combination of wit and handsomeness and sensuality that she could not possibly resist, and she didn't want to.

And now they would be holed up at the lake cottage for as long as the snow fell.

CHAPTER 8

The only thing the next twenty-four hours could be compared to was Christmas Eve and Christmas Day—arriving a couple of days early.

They had made it home almost without incident—though one of the turns in the road had been a bit scary in the snowy night. The power was still on at that point, and the cats were ready to assist with snuggles.

Vincent and Amy sat up for hours drinking hot lemon tea and talking as the snow fell, pausing only for kisses and caresses. Amy knew that her time with Vincent might be limited, but she felt drawn to enjoy the sweetness of getting to know this man, inch by inch. In that way, it felt like the future would never come, and she was perfectly content in the moment.

Midnight had adopted Vincent as her own, sliding up next to his lap with a chirp before lying down with her inky paws on his knee, purring, her eyes closed into little slits.

"It feels a million miles away from normal life, doesn't it?" he asked, gazing into her eyes and tracing her full lips with a gentle fingertip. He moved his finger aside and brushed his lips against hers.

"Except that it is real," she murmured, melting into him.

He whispered in her ear, "I want to enjoy you, slowly."

Amy took a deep breath, wishing she could just surrender to desire. "Things are heating up here."

"Need to pull back a bit?"

"Maybe," she said. "It's not that I don't want more—"

He stroked her cheek gently. "I get it. We'll take our time."

She smiled. "Yes. But we're only human, so I don't know if we'll take *that* much time."

They both chuckled, sheepish, still coming off of the high of desire.

Vincent moved to stand and reached for Amy's hand. "Time for bed? Think you can sleep?"

She yawned at the question. "It's *laaaaate*. We should get some sleep."

She moved to the window to look at the snow. It was still coming down. Her mother had texted earlier that she was all right, so that was a relief. But the bright whiteness continued to pile up under the moonlight. It was going to be a White Christmas, but was nature going a little overboard this year?

"I hope you're not in a rush to get out of here tomorrow either."

Vincent came up behind Amy to nuzzle the back of her neck. "Absolutely not."

"Good." She turned and put her arms around his neck. "Now kiss me goodnight."

*

Amy awoke to the familiar pressure of Larry against her hip, combined with the new furry presence of Midnight near her shoulder. Midnight liked to get in your face and nuzzle. What a little sweetie she was.

Amy was cozy under the duvet and blankets, and debated falling back asleep to prolong the comfort. But then she remembered that Vincent was sleeping on the living room sofa. He had chosen it over the spare bedroom so as to avoid interrupting Midnight's litterbox routine.

Amy smoothed her hair in the vanity mirror and tiptoed out to feed the cats. Vincent was snoozing on the sofa, breathing deeply. He couldn't be that comfortable, she thought. Maybe he just needed to rest from the stress of the last week and the lumpy sofa wasn't that big a deal.

She crossed to the window and surveyed the damage from last night's storm. More like a blizzard, it seemed. There must be a foot of snow—a lot for this part of the country. They might have to stay until Christmas, or close to it. It would all depend on how long it would take to clear the roads.

But the power was on, they had some supplies laid in, and there was nowhere else Amy wanted to be.

She fed the cats and looked in the kitchen for breakfast fixings. Let's see, toast, eggs, bacon. That should do it.

She texted her mom to check in, and mentioned that Vincent had slept on the sofa after being snowed in.

"Tell him I still don't like how he treated you! Love, Mom" her mother replied, followed by a somewhat inscrutable-looking series of emoji. Oh, Mom.

"I will, Mom. Stay safe, and let's check in later." What on earth did a dolphin emoji mean in this context?

"Sounds good. Love, Mom."

Vincent, it turned out, was such a heavy sleeper that he only awoke when the bacon was nearly prepared and the cats were yowling at Amy to share it with them.

She shook her head at the greedy pair. "You can't take down a pig, either of you. You absolutely haven't earned bacon." But Amy did take down a packet of tuna-flavored kitty treats and share them with the kitties.

"You probably couldn't catch a tuna either, little freeloaders." Vincent popped in and kissed her cheek, then placed his hand on her waist. He leaned in to smell Amy's hair. "Sleep well?"

She nodded. "Like a baby. How about you? That sofa isn't the most comfortable, I know."

"Nah, it's great. I've slept on so many air mattresses that leak out overnight that any cushion that sticks around is already an improvement."

He pulled some mugs down from the cupboard while she cooked. "Just milk, right?"

"Yes, there's some creamer in the fridge. Thanks. How would you like your eggs?"

"Oooh, how many ways can you make them?"

She looked up, trying to think of the answer. "Um, scrambled, omelet, over easy but half the time the yolks break. That might be it. I didn't go to culinary school."

"Me neither. I can't even do scrambled eggs properly, so maybe that's my request for today? Take pity on a poor scrambler."

Vincent took her into his arms and kissed her gently on the lips, drawing her close. She smelled wonderful, like sleep and traces of perfume. He wanted to lead her into the bedroom right then, but they had promised to move slowly.

Over breakfast, they debated how to spend their snow day.

"I have a short to-do list for today," Amy began. "Do you have more work responsibilities before Christmas?"

Vincent shook his head. "Not a one. I should call my parents with an update, though."

She nodded. "I'll keep checking in with my mom. I hope it'll warm up soon enough to avoid shoveling snow."

"That sounds wise. We can eat junk food and watch TV, or make snow angels, or take the cats for a walk, or—what?

"These cats would lose their sweet little minds if they were in the actual snow. Larry is so confused—look at him!"

It was true. Poor Miami native Larry was looking out at the snow, bobbing and weaving as though this strange new substance were going to attack him. Midnight, as a local cat, seemed a little more savvy, and had found a spot to sit, tuck up her paws, and observe the action.

"See, that's my lady Midnight right there," Vincent bragged. "I know Larry's your first love, but I like this ball of fluff right here."

Midnight looked up at Vincent, hearing the familiar sound of her name. She made a silent motion with her mouth, like a mute meow.

"That's right, kitty. I've got your back." Midnight knew she was being addressed and walked over to Vincent. He picked the fluffy creature up and held her on his lap for pets.

"There's something you can help me with on my to-do list if you're game."

"Of course, Amy. I'd love to help. What is it?"

"So every Christmas, my mom and I give to charity in small amounts. We call it microphilanthropy. When the weather's good, we withdraw some extra cash from the bank and tip extra everywhere, feed parking meters, all that stuff. It's like being Christmas elves."

"Oh, I love that idea. How do we do it when the weather, uh, sucks?"

"I was thinking about looking online for places to give, at least until the weather's better. Want to help me?"

"Right there with you."

They sat side by side on the sofa, each with their laptop, and snuggled up together. Between kisses they found a children's hospital to send treats to for the holiday, and a homeless shelter in Richmond that was going to use their donation that very night.

They also looked at a series of funding requests asking for help with medical bills or unemployment expenses, and gave some money to several families who hadn't received much of what they needed.

"That felt fantastic, Amy. I always give a little here and there, but something about setting aside time to do it means a lot to me."

"Aw, thanks. I know what you mean. It feels more personal when you are reading people's stories and knowing that you'll help them a little bit around the holidays."

"Has anyone ever done something like that for you?"

She smiled. No one had ever asked her that. "You know, no, but I'm open to it. Do you have anything in mind?"

"I am wondering what it will be. What's something you need?"

The energy in the room felt a little more serious now. "I think maybe I need to feel seen in some way. To feel acknowledged, recognized for what I do. My job is good, but it isn't *me*. I don't feel connected to it."

She hadn't thought about any of this herself before the words had spilled out, but it made perfect sense.

"It's hard to find something like that," Vincent admitted. "I got lucky and found something fairly compatible early on, but I still wonder what else is out there."

"No one ever tells you, growing up, how much of your adult life is spent still trying to figure things out. Finding a job, finding a way to advance and support yourself, finding a person, feeling fulfilled. And that's if you don't even have kids." Amy shook her head.

"I've wondered lately if I am doing the right thing by trying to simplify my life. Maybe I'm supposed to be okay with complicating it. What do you think?"

He seemed to expect an answer, but Amy wasn't sure she had one. "I feel like simplicity can be good, but not if you give up on genuine chances to be happy."

Now it was Vincent's turn to look serious. "Well, that's a weighty thing to think about, huh?"

They laughed, breaking the tension.

He stroked her back gently. "So we've solved the world's problems and we've identified our own. Is there anything left to do?"

She traced his lips with her finger before moving in for a kiss. Amy wasn't usually bold like this but Vincent seemed to welcome it. She wasn't sure how much longer she could hold out from more intimacy, especially stuck in the snow like this.

*

Later that day, they were snuggled on the sofa under both a blanket and the cats when a text from Lyra came in. Miami and those other parts of life seemed far away.

"We have to talk about Cabo! lmk when you can chat. Going for a run."

Amy had to laugh. She couldn't even open the door with this snow, let alone run outside.

"Something funny?" Vincent asked.

"I'm going to Mexico with a friend of mine in a few days, and she wants to talk about it."

His eyebrows arched in surprise. "Really? So this will all be a distant memory soon and you'll be warm on a beach."

"That's the idea. Distant, warm, and full of chips and salsa. Have you been to Mexico?"

"I have not," Vincent replied. "Some friends were trying to put a Spring Break trip to Cancún together when we were in college but it never happened."

"Why not?"

He smiled. "We were all broke and no one knew how to plan anything."

"Ha, I get it. I have a few friends like that. Planner friends are a nice change."

"Well," Vincent admitted. "It turns out that I am actually the planner friend. Didn't realize it until I started a business, but I have a knack for organizing things."

"We are a match, then, because I absolutely need planner friends to keep my life moving. I can do my job and handle my life, but time just creeps up on me and I find myself scrambling more often than I like to admit."

He leaned in seductively. "Would you like me to…look up some Cabo San Lucas restaurant reviews and send them to you for your trip?"

She laughed. "Honestly, I know you're joking, but yes."

After a minute, Amy looked at Vincent skeptically. "Wait. I thought you said you had no idea where to eat in town, and you were lost—"

He blushed lightly. "That comment might have been affected by the cute girl I ran into at the nursery."

"Oh, really? I have powers over you, I take it?"

"Maybe, maybe."

"What shall I do next? Are you taking orders?"

The teasing was such fun she didn't want it to end.

"Anything for you." He leaned over and kissed her, a moment of seriousness in the middle of play.

"Well, we have two tasks ahead of us: cooking dinner and starting a fire. Which would you like?"

"Hmmm. Could we do both at the same time?"

"What, cook in the fire?"

"Sure, in the fireplace, like when camping. Do you have anything that fits the bill?"

Amy was pleasantly surprised, if a little skeptical. "I have no idea, but I trust your judgment. I think."

A minute later, Vincent stood in the kitchen, contemplating the items in front of him: a package of hot dogs, some cornbread mix, and an iron skillet. "Um, Amy, are you okay with just having a fire and I'll cook this in the kitchen?"

She laughed from the next room. "Absolutely. Let's go against tradition. I'll light the fire and you make us something to eat. Then we'll take turns."

An hour later, they had finished their meal and were cozy by the fireplace, enjoying the scent of burning wood and the sound of crackling embers.

"I can't believe we're doing this again tomorrow," Vincent said, shaking his head in disbelief.

Amy had called up her mother earlier, because Rebecca always knew the latest town gossip. Apparently there were issues with getting plows working in town, and some folks had taken to shoveling the road in front of their houses to expedite the process.

"I think that's just ridiculous," Rebecca said. "I'm here, the cats are here with plenty of food.

We are all safe, and whenever we have Christmas, so be it."

"We'll have Christmas, mom, no worries. Not all of the presents will be here, but I still have a few things for Santa to give you."

"I just want you here to help me eat these cookies." Her mother chuckled. "How are things with Vincent? Is it too much being in one space?"

"It's going well. I'll fill you in when I see you. And the cats are so sweet together! Really, the weather is a nightmare but there are some Christmas miracles around, truly."

The evening passed happily. Vincent had found an old jigsaw puzzle in the hall closet and they were putting it together, watching a scene of a windmill in springtime take shape, bit by bit. Between the puzzle, and the crackling fire, and a hot mug of herbal tea, Amy couldn't ask for anything more.

When Vincent took a break to tidy up the kitchen, she started thinking she might want to invite him to sleep next to her tonight. Surely he could stay gentlemanly, and it *was* a cold winter night. They could cuddle up with the cats and sleep in tomorrow.

She saw his phone light up with a text. Without thinking she glanced over at it, thinking she'd let him know who texted so he could reply.

The text was from Karrie. It said, "I love you, too."

Amy recoiled. She shouldn't have snooped in the first place, so she couldn't say anything. She felt terrible. Had he been texting Karrie that he loved her while the two of them were enjoying this idyllic day together?

Her thoughts raced, trying to come up with a logical explanation. She decided to wait and see how Vincent reacted to the text.

"Back!" Vincent came in a few minutes later.

"Hey, thanks for tidying up!" She managed what she hoped was a reassuring smile. Amy picked up a puzzle piece, unable to concentrate, but still able to pretend she was looking for its place in the puzzle.

He leaned over and kissed her forehead.

She saw him look over at his phone and check the text. Vincent silently pocketed the phone and looked at Amy, not breaking concentration. What was going on?

"Everything okay?" she ventured.

"Yeah, just work. They liked the photos!"

He was lying! Oh, come on. Why was this happening? She needed to focus on the puzzle or she'd give away that she had seen Karrie's text. They were still stuck in the snow, and spending the rest of the night arguing was not something Amy had the energy to do. There was a fire, there was a puzzle, and he was good company even if she was realizing, with pangs of regret, that Vincent couldn't be the person for her.

Larry peeped up at Amy from the ground. She scooped him up into her lap and calmed herself by petting him. He purred loudly and even drooled a little onto her sleeve.

"Awww, that's a good boy."

Vincent looked at her, more seriously. "You doing okay? You seem a little tense."

Amy didn't want to have this conversation now. "I'm probably just sleepy. Maybe head off to bed in a few?"

Later that night, she lay in her bed wondering if there were a good reason for that kind of exchange. There had to be. Maybe his ex-girlfriend was responding to something, and trying to win him back, she said she loved him. It was that "too" that absorbed her mind. But he *must* be a good person. The alternative seemed so unlikely.

*

The following morning was Christmas Eve. They sat down with coffee, and Vincent seemed to be scanning Amy's eyes for a clue. He knew something was amiss. And she knew she needed to say something.

"So have you heard from Karrie? Your ex? I'm still feeling a little worried about that situation." She exhaled. She didn't say she had accidentally snooped and seen Vincent's phone, but she'd also told the truth.

He nodded. "Yeah, I've heard a bit from her. I don't like to lay all of my baggage on you, but she is sending a lot of texts."

Okay, this was good; this was an honest reply. "What kind?" she asked.

"To be honest, they aren't super coherent. 'I hate you!' 'I love you!' "Here's why we would never work!' 'Here's why we can't stay apart!' I can't even follow the communication."

She laughed, somewhat relieved. "I saw your phone going off a lot last night and was kind of worried, but didn't want to start anything up in case I was wrong."

"Here, I'll act it out for you—" he grabbed his phone and unlocked the screen.

Amy put her hands over her ears. "No, no! I don't want to know."

Vincent moved the phone over to her. "You asked for it, Amy!"

He held the phone in front of Amy and scrolled it in front of her. Every single text was from Karrie. One after another. Not a single reply from Vincent, with an "I love you" or otherwise.

"She's been talking to herself?" That was odd, but she had seen stranger things happen.

He nodded. "It's unfortunate. She's, uhhh, not the best at social cues." He shrugged. "I know she'll find the right person for her, but boy, that is not me." He winked one of his soft amber eyes at her.

Amy smiled. "I don't know, maybe I've been talking to myself a little bit, too." She kind of *had,* now that she was thinking about it. Talking herself out of this connection, talking herself back into it.

She took hold of his hand and they sat together for a minute.

Vincent broke the silence. "You know what would hit just right with this coffee?"

Before she could answer, he was in the kitchen. In a moment, he returned with a plate of Christmas cookies.

Their eyes met, and both were clearly thinking about something more than Christmas cookies.

"Don't mind if I do," Amy said with a wink.

"Maybe we should take a little break together after our fortifying cookie breakfast," Vincent said, his eyes gesturing to the bedroom.

She giggled. "That sounds perfect to me."

CHAPTER 9

At dinnertime on Christmas Eve, Amy looked around her at the dinner table, unable to believe how she had been so lucky.

To her left was her mother, Rebecca, who was safe and easy to visit now that the roads to the lake were cleared of snow. She smiled, herself grateful to see her daughter, safe, sound, and—from the looks of it—falling in love with the ruggedly handsome man from the nursery.

To Amy's right was Vincent, engaged in conversation with her mother. The two both loved nature photography and Rebecca was only too pleased to have a kindred spirit to chat with her about shutter speeds and rare bird sightings.

"I keep telling Amy she should go birding with me, but she never listens. What a stubborn girl I've raised—you might be in for some trouble, Vincent!"

He smiled. "I don't mind a little stubbornness—it means she stands up for herself."

He touched her knee gently under the table, and Amy felt herself blush a little. She recovered enough to reply. "You know, Mom, I might go birding with you if you threw in a few compliments once in a while."

"Well," added Vincent, "to spread the compliments around a bit, this is a fantastic roast beef. It's such a wonderful treat, and the fixings are perfect with it."

They all regarded the tabletop spread, which included peas, mashed potatoes, and her grandmother's recipe for Yorkshire pudding—the savory popovers that the family had enjoyed for Christmas Eve for as long as they could remember. New this year was a fresh cucumber salad with a tart dressing—something tangy to balance the heavy meal.

"I love this salad too, Mom. Is it a new recipe?"

Her mother shook her head no. "I don't have much that is fresh right now, but the herb garden still manages to produce a little in the winter. So I used the cucumbers I picked up the other day, some chives, and some fresh tarragon, all in a mustard vinaigrette."

"Well, it's delicious," Vincent echoed. "I love how it sets off the other ingredients. We usually have ham at Christmas back home, so this whole setup is pretty new to me."

"We do ham for Easter, but I think we've had it for Christmas in the past?" Amy looked at her mother quizzically.

"Yes, that's true." Rebecca recalled. "However, we tend to start a ham at Christmas breakfast and graze on it for the rest of the day."

"That's right! I remember dad eating ham sandwiches all day and spoiling his appetite." Amy laughed at this new recollection.

"I mostly remember having to keep the ham hidden from the pets." Her mother shook her head. "We mustn't linger too long at the table. Those foster cats are probably going crazy cooped up like that."

It was always much easier to keep the cats out of the dining room for an hour than it was to shoo them away every time one wanted to make a jump for the table.

"Well, you can hardly blame the cats for wanting such a delicious meal," Vincent said. "Why don't I put the leftovers away and you two can catch up?"

"Well, aren't you just the best?" Amy smiled and kissed Vincent gently on the cheek as his arm slid around her waist. She was indeed a lucky person this Christmas.

*

Later that evening, the three were cozy on the sofa, drinking hot spiced cider and listening to Christmas carols while they chatted and watched the glow of the Christmas tree. The gray kitten, Ash, slept in a tiny circle on the largest cat bed, dreaming of treats and toys from Santa Cat.

"How are things at your parents' house this holiday?" Rebecca asked Vincent.

"Well, they miss me a little, sure, but they seem to enjoy spending time together. I suppose I'm lucky in that regard. Not a perfect childhood, we had our problems. But also there were none of those 'Take my wife, please!' jokes in my house. I know that's more than a lot of people can say."

Amy nodded. "I know what you mean. My parents were close like that." She glanced at her mother. "I'm sorry, Mom. I know this time is hard."

Rebecca brushed it off. "No, no. This is when we are supposed to remember the past. Holidays keep people we love with us even when they aren't here anymore." She reached down to pet a kitten who perched near her foot. "When I sleep at night there are always kitties to cuddle, and all day long, so many little beings depend on me. It's okay to be sentimental sometimes. You can't push it all down inside."

Amy nodded. She had tried to suppress her sadness to some extent with Conrad, and it hadn't worked. She had also been reticent with Vincent, and that was not helpful either. Just feel the feelings, Amy, she thought to herself. Vincent reached an arm around her and held her gently.

"I agree, Rebecca," he replied. "I can't think of a feeling so scary that people can't just tell one another what's on their mind. Perhaps I've just been lucky."

Amy smiled. "I hope you don't know someone who's all *that* terrifying."

Vincent laughed, "well, we all knew a weirdo or two in school, I imagine. There was a guy in my dorm who used dog shampoo in the shower room, and I once ran track with a guy who everyone said killed a guy at his last school."

There was an awkward pause. "Do you think he did it?" Amy asked, genuinely curious.

"He was a very slow runner," Vincent thought as he spoke. "They would have caught him, no doubt." He winked.

"Perhaps he started the rumor so that everyone would think he was a faster runner?" Rebecca suggested, giggling.

"You two!" Amy smiled. "I want to know what happened to the dog shampoo guy."

"Actually, he ended up making a ton of money in Silicon Valley. Maybe he'll write a memoir and explain when some of his stranger choices."

"I imagine he's saved a lot of it, too, if he's still using pet products in his hair."

Vincent laughed. "Could be. When he— Jason, that's his name--was hired out of college they sent some fancy movers to move him out of his dorm room—real white-glove service for just some kid in a dorm, that's how good a computer science major he was. Turns out all he had was his gaming computer and a duffel bag of his things, so these movers who've probably moved Picassos must have been *very* disappointed."

"Oh my! He sounds like a real character." Amy and her mother agreed. Rebecca continued, "You know Amy, if you hadn't met Vincent here,

I'd suggest this Jason person for you. You work in technology!"

"I don't think I'm on his level, Mom!" Amy joked. "Besides, Vincent didn't even say his friend was single."

Her mother raised an eyebrow. "He uses dog shampoo, Amy. I'm guessing he was a late bloomer."

Vincent smiled. "You are correct, Rebecca. Maybe someday I'll invite him out here to visit. It's a pleasant town, and I'm not afraid of a little competition. Amy, what do you think?"

She couldn't help but be amused. "At least wait until the New Year, Vincent! I couldn't possibly handle his level of romance. But I promise I'll be ready to howl at the moon by then."

"You're leaving town in a couple of days anyway, though, right?"

"I am indeed. I am enjoying this holiday so very much, but I can't lie—I am going to enjoy the Pacific Ocean and a margarita with my bestie just as much."

"Be careful you don't get swept away by some *gauchito* out there!" her mother teased.

"Does that mean a *miniature cowboy*, mom? Like a tiny horse with a cowboy doll strapped to it?" They didn't speak Spanish very well, but had tried to converse over the years, often hilariously incorrectly.

Vincent interjected. "I promise to be better than all of the sizes of cowboy."

"Oh, do you?" Amy flirted. "I'll hold you to that. Just keep using human products and fight off the tiny cowboys, and you'll be the most eligible man I know."

They were all beyond silly by this point. "We need to settle down, y'all, please," Rebecca insisted. They hadn't even opened their Christmas Eve gifts.

"Okay, Mom's right. We have to open a present now, then head home before midnight."

The first Christmas miracle that day had been the clear roads that enabled them to travel into town. And the second miracle had been this, tonight—each person had presents to open.

Amy gave a gift to her mother and a gift to Vincent. Vincent had *somehow* found gifts for her and her mother, and Rebecca had a present for her daughter as well as for Vincent. The three looked surprised and delighted that each had gifts from the others.

Rebecca went first and opened a pair of soft, magenta fleece slipper socks. The socks were a traditional gift from Amy each year, but Rebecca loved the new vibrant color and the chance to think of her daughter's kindness whenever she wanted to get warmer. Next she opened her gift from Vincent: a container of gourmet cocoa mix—just right for these chilly nights. "You're both so thoughtful—thank you!"

Vincent opened his next. Rebecca had bought him a bottle of whiskey—something she used to do for Amy's father each Christmas Eve. She couldn't help but smile at the sweetness of the gesture, which Vincent enjoyed for other reasons. "We'll have to try a bit as a nightcap when we get back!" he said as he read the label. From Amy there was a simple present—a mug with a "V" on it. "Any time you're at the lake house, you'll have your own mug to enjoy. Also I had no clue what to buy you, and Target had cute mugs—"

Vincent shushed her. "No, shh, don't worry. I love it. I promise. I had to buy mine at the grocery store so really, don't feel bad." He handed Amy her gift. She felt its familiar weight in her hands and realized what it was before she opened the wrapper.

Amy read the label of the bag of coffee beans. "Sumatra—of course. Well, I have a few new favorites now, don't I?"

*

As they returned to the lake cottage with Vincent driving, Amy looked out the window. The snow was melting a little, but clung to the leaves by the side of the road and the hills beyond. It might not be the snowiest Christmas, but it would still be a White Christmas if it held on a little. She loved the brightness the snow added to the night drive.

"When are you going to catch up with your parents?" she asked Vincent.

"Hmm. They tend to sleep in on Christmas Day, now that there aren't kids in the house anymore."

"Aww, were you one of those naughty children who woke up their parents at dawn on Christmas Day?"

"I didn't know they were up late putting together presents—I thought they were just slow in the morning." He laughed.

"Well, the cats will enjoy their revenge by waking you up at six tomorrow, demanding to be fed." She placed her hand on his arm, patting it gently.

"I'm pretty sure those cats are coming right for you in the morning, young lady."

Ordinarily, Amy didn't enjoy being called a "young lady," or "honey," or those other old-fashioned nicknames for women that men sometimes used. But something in the way Vincent teased her as he said it made Amy feel cherished and content. It was just silly banter, and he clearly respected her.

For a second, Amy wondered whether they were moving too fast, but then she reconsidered. She had clearly been suspicious of Vincent, had had her guard up, but how long could she go on this way? She couldn't live her whole life with her heart locked away. Love meant taking a leap of faith, trusting in the unknown. Her heart had survived Conrad's attempts to break it, hadn't it?

Like Mary Hatch and George Bailey, perhaps they were on their way to fall in love. She hoped so.

*

At bedtime, they stood outside her bedroom doorway, holding each other in the dim evening light. Vincent leaned down and kissed Amy slowly and gently, yet still passionately.

She clutched his back with her hands and leaned to whisper in his ear. "You feel so good."

He held her face in his hands and sighed. "I'm so lucky you gave me another chance, Amy. I don't want to stop touching you, or leave this room, or anything. I want to freeze time right here."

Both of them paused as if that were exactly what happened, memorizing the cottage, the quiet, and the electricity between them.

Vincent kissed her again, deeply this time. Amy instinctively pressed against him, her hand stroking the place on his back between the shoulder blades.

Their hands moved more insistently now, each wanting to touch and know the other.

Then, slowly, their intent shifted. The touch that originally surveyed his body now aimed to please it. Vincent's hand found a place just under her collarbone that Amy had barely known existed. Now it was all she could think of, his gentle touch, his lips grazing her upper chest, the strength of his back under her hands.

It was so new and so intoxicating that Amy led Vincent by the hand into the bedroom with complete confidence. It was time to take a chance.

CHAPTER 10

There were no sleigh bells on the roof that night, and there were no stockings hung by the chimney with care, but Amy and Vincent still awoke to magic on Christmas morning. The cats, snuggled up to them, purred and kneaded their humans.

Those humans had certainly stayed up late the night before, wanting to kiss and touch one another, barely able to hold back from consummating the relationship. Amy wasn't prudish, but she still wanted to wait just a little longer. Vincent respectfully complied, though she sensed he would be ready whenever she was.

He held her palm to his lips and kissed it. She leaned over and smiled. "Good morning, sleepyhead."

"Merry Christmas, Ms. Amy." Vincent squeezed her hand and released it. He turned to pet Midnight, who seemed happy curled up by his side.

For his part, Larry was sprawled on Amy's chest, his large belly soft and vulnerable. She was tempted to give Larry a belly rub, but didn't want to rile him up too early in the morning. Larry liked a belly rub for about half a second, but then he liked to kick and bite as though he were play-fighting.

She giggled at the sight of them all. "I have no idea what to do with the lot of us for Christmas morning—what a silly crew we make."

"Besides, the cats don't really pull their weight around here. Just living on the company dime, isn't that right?" Vincent scratched Midnight's ears, which pleased her immensely. The black cat started to wriggle playfully. He scooped her up for a snuggle.

"She seems to have adopted you," Amy observed. "I'm glad I could introduce you."

Larry sniffed Amy's nose as she leaned over to him. "Awww, you're a good man, Mr. Larry Guillaume. Sorry, Mr. Man-cat." Larry chirped back, then jumped down in search of food.

Amy peered through the doorway into the living room. "So we didn't do very much to decorate last night, but we can certainly spruce things up around here a bit, maybe start a fire."

"Fantastic—I'll take care of the fire if you want to figure out food. Or at least coffee." Vincent did look a little worn out. She liked having worn him out, though.

"Perfect." She leaned in and kissed him quickly.

*

After a hearty breakfast—pancakes and maple syrup, with local bacon—and a lot of coffee, Amy was feeling refreshed. She looked away from the roaring fire and surveyed the gray skies, the lake, and the hills beyond. The snow would be gone in a day or so, but there was just enough white left on the hills to lend some beauty to the day.

Vincent was in the shower, and Amy called her mother to check in on her.

"Good morning! Merry Christmas!"

"Awww, Merry Christmas, Amy! How's the lake looking today?"

"Still a bit of snow out, but the roads are clear. Did you eat yet?"

"I did—just made an omelet! Do you want to come here, or would you like me to come over there?"

Amy looked around her. She didn't want to douse the roaring fire, or leave it unattended. Maybe her mother missed this kind of cozy time at the lake?

"We have a fire going here—why don't you come by and check on Midnight and Larry? Maybe there's a Christmas movie on. I still have some cookies—" It was a different suggestion, but maybe now was the time for new traditions.

"That sounds marvelous! I have some dinner things I can bring—some wine as well? We can have treats and presents by the lake."

Amy nodded. "I'm excited! We could use a little variety once in a while."

"Oh, and Santa came for you last night, so don't worry—I have that covered!"

"Okay, great, Mom—well, we'll see you in—an hour?"

They hung up. Amy snuggled into the throw on the sofa, her feet tucked up under her. She wiggled her toes in her socks. The fire hissed and crackled. She could get used to this.

She heard Vincent getting ready in the spare room. His feet made shadowy spots on the floor under the doorway. She wondered what they would do tonight, but then realized she didn't even care. It would be time with this person, this one who might be *her* person.

He opened the door and walked out of the guest room. To her surprise, his suitcase was packed and ready to go.

"Hey, what's up?" Amy hoped her face looked genuinely perplexed and not annoyed. She was trying not to make assumptions.

Vincent didn't seem surprised by her expression. "Just packed up to head to my parents' house. Should make it in time for Christmas dinner."

"Okay. You didn't mention that you were leaving right now, so I'm a little surprised." She tried to seem neutral.

A silence hung between them.

"Not sure what you want me to say, Amy. They're my parents. Of course I'm spending Christmas with them." He wasn't making eye contact with her.

Had she missed something? "Yes, absolutely. I must have lost track of time."

Vincent seemed upset now. She didn't know whether he was the type who liked more time to himself when he was upset, or whether he preferred to talk. Amy decided to be cautious and give him some space. He seemed touchy.

He was moving more quickly now, still avoiding eye contact.

"Here, I'll take a look in my room and see if you left anything—"

Might as well be helpful. She found his glasses and a half-empty glass of water and handed over the former while the latter went into the sink to be washed later.

He had finished packing and seemed ready to go.

"Here, let me send you out with your present." She handed him the small bag she'd filled with a few surprises.

"Oh, right, umm." He looked awkward and strangely hurried, considering that he had plenty of time to get to where he was going.

This really was odd. They'd exchanged presents the night before. He had something for her as well, didn't he? "Well, you can take it with you if you'd like." Amy waited for his response.

"Yes, well, thanks. I appreciate it." He leaned over and kissed her on the cheek. "I'll call you—"

And just like that, he was gone.

Wow. She couldn't believe it. He seemed to have turned on a dime, and she had no idea what had happened. Clearly something was up, and Vincent didn't want to tell her about it.

Amy looked at the living room. She saw the second coffee cup, the second napkin, the little bits of evidence that Vincent had been there.

She had responded peacefully to him but was increasingly becoming more irritated. He hadn't bought her a Christmas present. He had said nothing about his departure until he had packed his bags. She was sure of it. And Vincent's demeanor toward her had turned cold so quickly.

This was too many coincidences for her mind, Amy thought to herself. There had been too many incidents with Vincent. She felt like she was making excuses for someone she didn't really know yet. A lot of women loved mysterious men, but this seemed like a lot of work. Yes, he was handsome and broody, but what explanation could account for the rest of his strange behavior?

There would be no Amy and Vincent, she decided. The highs were perfect, she had to admit, but he was too difficult to read and not a good communicator. What on earth *was* that exchange as he left? An impersonal peck on the cheek from someone who'd slept beside her the night before. Merry Christmas, indeed.

*

"But why did he leave so suddenly?" Rebecca wondered later. "It just doesn't make sense."

Amy shook her head and looked at her mother. "I'd be a fool to ignore the messages, though. He didn't tell me about his ex before, either; he just bailed and acted like I was the weirdo for asking him questions."

Her mother shrugged and picked up the fireplace poker. The dying embers sparked a bit more. "You're not wrong. What will you do if he tries to get back together?"

"I don't know. If we were in the same place for longer, this would all feel much easier. Should we put another log on the fire?" Before she could speak more, her mother shushed her. She retrieved a couple of logs from the logpile and arranged them in the fireplace.

Amy helped, picking up the bellows. She gave a little boost to the embers, hoping the bellows would help the new wood catch fire.

"Looks good," Amy declared, satisfied. "I don't know what I'll do if he reaches out again," she mused. "I'm certainly not going to wait around for Vincent. He seemed pretty eager to get out of here earlier today. Unless there's something important happening and he reaches out to make amends, I must walk away."

"I think that's a good call. Know your boundaries, Amy." Rebecca gathered their teacups and headed to the kitchen. "Shall we switch from tea to wine? I bought some charcuterie we can set up. You look like you could use some cheese."

Amy laughed. "I don't know of any problems that cheese can't fix."

Larry entered the room as if on cue. Midnight soon followed. "It's like they can hear us talking about food."

"You are greedy little gremlins, Larry and Midnight. You're meant for each other, though." Amy smiled.

"They clearly are a lovely couple," her mother echoed. "If nothing else happens, at least those two are a love match."

"I love watching them together, Mom. Thank you for giving me the nudge to take Midnight in."

Her mother leaned in for a hug. "Why don't I set us up a plate and you can find a nice movie to watch, hon?"

Amy wanted to tear up. No one took care of her like her mom did. She nodded and returned to her favorite spot on the sofa. She would enjoy every second of being cared for.

Rebecca brought Amy a plate of charcuterie and cheese, with sliced baguette, olives, and all the fixings. Together they cozied up in front of the revitalized fire, drinking a plummy pinot noir. "Let's do gifts afterwards? That way we'll space it all out, right?" Amy wanted to make the good parts of this day last as long as they could.

"Mom, I'm sorry."

"Whatever for?"

"This trip was supposed to be for us to stay together, not for me to ditch you for some guy."

Rebecca laughed. "I practically shoved you at him, honey. And besides, you said you'd be here through New Year's after your trip."

Cabo! That's right. Oh, what a good idea that had been. Lyra was the best for organizing this trip. They had been texting intermittently over the last few days but still needed to fit in a long video chat to go over the details before departure.

"That's true, Mom. Maybe we can do something fun together around the New Year. No men, just fun."

Her mother contemplated this idea. "You know, this sounds silly but I always wanted to try the new indoor mini golf place that's off the road near Richmond. The other cat ladies aren't interested, and it feels unseemly to play mini golf alone."

Amy laughed. It was such a small request. "Absolutely. We will mini golf until we have golfed every color ball."

They clinked their wine glasses. "Let me top that up, Amy." Her mother refilled her glass while Amy scrolled through the channels on the TV. "Still need a distraction?"

Amy nodded quickly. She kept becoming anxious and stuck in her head whenever the conversation slowed. "Thanks, Mom. Besides, this way we can save all the presents for the end and they're always so much fun."

"This way it might feel like we have a second Christmas Eve."

"Oh that's it! Go Mom!" Rebecca looked askance at Amy. "No, I mean let's use tonight to re-do last night, when you-know-who was with us."

"Amy, I think that's a—" Amy wasn't sure how her mother would complete this sentence, and her mother looked a little unsure herself. "—a brilliant idea. They're just days, and we can even do stockings in the morning. Tonight is Christmas Eve, then."

Amy raised her glass. "To Christmas Eve. Whatever happened last night, that was *not* Christmas Eve."

They had a cozy evening watching *Home Alone* and laughing together over the film's slapstick humor and heartwarming reunion of a mother and her child. That night, each went to bed feeling peaceful.

Amy had shut down her phone hours before. Everyone she needed to hear about was in this house, and everyone else in the family could call her mother in case of a true emergency. She was sure there were messages but they could wait on this of all days.

*

They called the next day "new Christmas," and spent it sleeping in, drinking their coffee with real cream, and opening little stocking gifts from Santa. This was their favorite part of Christmas, and it was worth the day's wait.

Amy and Rebecca pulled chocolates and gummi bears from their Christmas stockings, as well as pens and lip balms. For years, Rebecca had bought Amy a roll of the candy loops she liked best, and Amy always looked forward to the treat. Amy had found some herbal tea for her mother's stocking, as well as a face mask and some hand cream.

Because they were so occupied with opening their little gifts—and playing with the cats, who loved all the ribbons and bows that came with the unwrapping of presents—Amy and her mother had spent half the day on these gifts and chatting before they realized it.

"I wished I could have done this sort of thing with my mother," Rebecca said. "She was always so busy with us, and then was always taking care of her husband, and then I had you, and it always seemed like there were people surrounding her. Until one day, there weren't."

Amy nodded. They were a small family, and that was lonely sometimes, but she was grateful for this time. "I'm glad we could do this, Mom."

"You know, I won't judge you if you need to get back to your phone and all. We are having fun, but you have work catchup to do I imagine. And of course, if you want to unblock or unmute or whatever you call it, you-know-who—"

"Yeah, about that. I should probably at least see if there was anything he had to say, and also look at work." Amy booted up her laptop and her telephone.

"You do that and I'll work on my puzzles." While Amy loved her online crossword puzzle, her mother liked to do sudoku puzzles in a big paper book. "Keeps my brain sharp," she said.

First, the work emails. She wanted to avoid Vincent's message if there was one, but Amy also knew that if she didn't check work first, she might have a hard time concentrating if there were some major personal messages.

Work wasn't bad, thankfully. She'd have to work for a couple of hours later that night on some of the post-Christmas late-night sales, but she tended to enjoy that part.

Now the phone. There were three texts and a photo:

The photo was of her gifts to him—a stocking filled with sweets and cookies, coffee, mini liqueurs, and other treats. The larger gift was an insulated travel mug with images from the lake etched in the stainless steel. The accompanying text said, "Thanks a bunch!!" with a smiley emoji. Okay. That was expected.

Then the other texts: "Some unexpected things at my parents' house" and "Hope it was a good Christmas for you."

Okay. She thought to herself, perhaps that's why he left in such a hurry. As before, they barely knew one another. She exhaled at length. Apparently she'd been tense, holding her breath while reading the texts. Midnight hopped up beside her for some pets and head scritches. "Aww, sweet kitty. Here's a little love." Amy smiled down at the fluffy black cat.

She texted back. "Thanks! Enjoy your visit." Then set down the phone. Then picked up the phone, silenced the volume, and put it down again. She'd said what she had to. She was polite but didn't encourage more conversation. That, as they say, is that.

Amy popped back on to her laptop to video chat with Lyra. Her mother joined in to say hello.

"Amyyyyyyy!" Lyra smiled from her cameraphone. "It's tomorrrrrroowwwwwww!" She did a little happy dance. "We are going to be drinking a margarita and eating as much guacamole as we can this time tomorrow."

"Maybe I can come, too!" Rebecca joked.

"Next time you should join us," Amy replied. "Maybe when you're in between fostering cats we will have a quick getaway."

"I would love that!" her mother smiled.

"If we find any handsome older men, we'll make sure to give them your number, Rebecca," Lyra teased.

"I'm done with that, thank you very much, but I hope you girls have fun." Amy's mother headed into the kitchen to make some tea so the younger women could chat.

"So what's going on with that guy, Amy?" Lyra knew how to be direct, that was for sure.

"It's not happening. Kind of a shame, but there were mixed signals and then he sort of took off on Christmas." Amy was getting better at talking about it, so that was good.

"People are weird during the holidays. Maybe you'll run into him again, or maybe we'll find you some stunner when we're out dancing?"

"I might be more into hammock and beach time than dancing but I'll see if I can rally."

"Understood. Okay, so first night I was thinking we meet at the hotel and get dinner there? That way we won't need reservations and apparently it's right on the water—" Lyra continued, her superior planning skills on display. Amy was always comforted that her friend was so put-together in all respects.

"This will be so relaxing, Lyra. Thank you for pushing me to leave my house."

"One of these days I'll come up to your lake house and just…sleep for a week."

Amy laughed. "I'm pretty sure you'd find some mischief or other to occupy you. Not sure where you'd find it around here, but I believe in you."

Lyra gave a little salute from her camera. Amy responded with finger guns. Lyra rolled her eyes at the corniness.

They said their goodbyes, both feeling cheered. Amy and Rebecca cozied up to have a little tea and go over plans for feeding Larry and Midnight during Amy's trip. Larry and Midnight were present for the discussion, curled up on the braided vintage rug in front of the fireplace.

Her mother headed home to take care of her own cats and handle some things around the house. Amy patted the place on the sofa next to her. The cats looked up at her sleepily. Larry returned to his dreams of birds and mice, but Midnight moved a little closer to Amy. She settled at her feet, still near Larry, but offering comfort to her new human. She was such a sweet cat. Amy worked on her laptop a little longer, making sure the next few days were clear and covered for her at work. That way her vacation could actually be a vacation.

Her phone showed a missed call from Vincent and another text. "I wanted to check in, but I know you're traveling. Let me know when you're back in town." So he was still interested, then?

This was not good communication from his end. Was she also communicating poorly? She wondered. She scrolled back through their texts. She had been a little terse with him on occasion, but nothing malicious. And she hadn't led him in strange, conflicting directions with ex-girlfriends and sudden departures and the like. She was just being herself.

Okay. Deep breath. This was the last chance, and only because she felt so connected to Vincent when they were together. One text and she'd lay it on the line. Then she was willing to walk away.

"Vincent, it hurt my feelings that you left so suddenly. If we were to try dating, I would need better communication and more trust in your honesty and consistent actions. If that interests you, please let me know. I care about you and I'm willing to try if you are. xo Amy." And, send. She watched the little check mark appear beside her text. Okay then. I guess *that* was that.

She liked this new version of herself. She was advocating for herself and still doing fun things. She was also still willing to put herself out there. Amy thought about the parts of Vincent that were hard to find elsewhere. He was driven in his career, creative, funny, handsome, tall, fit— definitely a catch. But for now, there were swimsuits and sundresses to pack and an alarm to set for an early morning flight.

CHAPTER 11

She was up at the crack of dawn to drive to her small regional airport. As was customary in the Southeast, Amy had to change planes in Atlanta for her flight to Mexico. She knew, however, that by the time she was in the air it would be the afternoon and she'd be energized for the vacation.

The most exciting part of the flight, by far, was being upgraded to business class with some old frequent flier miles she hadn't used. There was a ton of room, and she felt like a rockstar with the extra amenities—and lounge access.

During her layover, Amy enjoyed some snacks in the Atlanta lounge, and sat down with a glass of sparkling wine. She did a little work on her laptop—deleting old emails, saving things into folders—and felt like a fancy executive. Maybe she actually was fancy, though she didn't feel like it. Director of late-night programming did sound special, come to think of it, even if the paycheck wasn't massive.

She finished her wine and scoped out the rest of the lounge. There were even showers here. She wondered whether there was a surcharge for the showers. The attendant assured her that there was not, and Amy decided that she'd use the next half hour to stand under a steaming hot shower before crawling into another plane seat. Perhaps the shower would even help her stay hydrated.

It sure felt good to wash off the sweat from her first flight and use the fragrant eucalyptus bodywash the airline had provided. She could get used to this business-class lounge, most definitely.

Amy settled in for her four-hour flight, of which she hoped to enjoy every moment. She drank a mimosa while waiting for takeoff—hoping the juice would minimize the effects of the alcohol—then switched to sparkling water with lime for the rest of the flight.

She reclined her seat fully, knowing the person behind her wouldn't be affected, and watched a movie as she sipped her cool drink. The film was a Christmas-themed romantic comedy Amy had seen years ago. There were no surprises and a happy ending, so it was the perfect selection. This was the perfect journey to heal her heart.

Lunch was light, some prosciutto with melon as a starter, then a Caesar salad and a pasta dish. There was also a large wrapped shortbread cookie, but she decided to save that in case there was an issue with food later. Once, long ago, Amy had arrived at a rural hotel ten minutes after the kitchen had closed. The only option for calories had been root beer from a vending machine, and she swore never to arrive at a hotel emptyhanded again.

She napped lightly at the end of the film and woke up just as the plane was descending into Cabo San Lucas. There were no calls, and no texts. There had been total quiet on the plane. She was already feeling better, and couldn't wait to catch up with Lyra for a few days.

*

The flight had been like an escape, but Cabo seemed to be a whole world away. Their resort was on the ocean, nestled between the beach and the mountains. Lyra was waiting outside.

"Woooo! We're here!"

They hugged excitedly. Lyra pulled back from the hug, looked at Amy, and said: "I have to hear absolutely everything that happened with this guy."

The room was peaceful and tastefully-decorated, with soothing creamy tones and what was clearly a recent renovation. They even had a blocked view of the Pacific Ocean but was still worth the splurge because of the private plunge pool on their balcony.

Lyra investigated the amenities while Amy unpacked. "Wait a minute—" she paused as she retrieved a small bottle from the console table. "There's free tequila here, Amy!"

"Wait a minute, free-free?"

"Yes, it says to enjoy this local tequila with our compliments. And there are little glasses."

"They want us to do shots. Here." Amy looked around her at their luxe surroundings before she began to giggle.

Lyra was pouring tequila for both. "We shouldn't just leave it, Amy. That would be rude." She winked and handed her friend a small pour.

They toasted and took small sips. It felt more civilized, and they wanted to taste whether this tequila was special in some way. Amy admitted she couldn't tell the difference.

"Yeah, I don't really get it either," Lyra nodded. "Now tell me about this Vincent."

Amy let out a longer, louder sigh than she had intended. Clearly she must be working through a few lingering feelings.

They caught up on gossip as they unpacked and sipped, Lyra listening and processing the stories about Vincent with careful attention.

"I honestly can't tell about this guy," Lyra replied. "They tell you that mixed signals just means the guy isn't into you, and I tend to go with that in my own life."

"I was wondering the same thing, even though it is kind of an ego blow." Amy shrugged. "I guess it's hard to predict attraction."

"But the thing is," Lyra said, "he is attracted to you. Right?"

Amy nodded. "It seemed so! And he enjoys talking with me. He went out of his way to pursue me, then it seemed like he ran away."

"What did he text you back after your big confession?"

"Um, I turned off notifications from him. I just wanted to calm down a bit in case he was rude or dismissive."

"Want me to check?" Lyra reached out her hand for the phone. Amy unlocked her phone and handed it over. Lyra scrolled through the text messages. She read one and nodded.

"What is it?" Amy was nervous.

"Here, you can read it. It isn't bad." Lyra handed back the phone.

Amy read. "I'm still very interested in you, Amy. There are a few things about my family that I haven't told you, but if you'll give me a chance to fill you in when I get back, I'll try to make it up to you. I'm sorry for being closed-off. Text or call anytime."

Huh. So there was something he didn't want to talk about, but now he was willing to be more open. Amy looked pleadingly at Lyra, who shrugged.

"Amy, I think it's a good sign, but it all depends on what the family stuff is. Like is there an identical twin who's been swapping places?"

Amy laughed in spite of herself. "Yeah, that makes sense. What other movie clichés could it be? Is he secretly ill and doesn't want to hurt my feelings? Is there a secret baby he inherited?" They were both giggling now.

"No, Amy, he's a spy in the Witness Protection Program. But for real, though, what's the worst thing he could be?"

"Married!" She wasn't wrong. "But he isn't. There's no trace of anyone except an ex-girlfriend who broke it off a while back."

Lyra looked off out the window, deep in thought.

"Lyra, what's up?"

"I kind of need to eat something. Should we get chips and guac down by the resort pool, or here, in our room, by the room pool?"

"These are such hard decisions," Amy replied, playing along. "And there's also a beach, and a firepit. There are simply too many places to eat chips here."

"Let's start in the room, shall we? And we can soak in the plunge pool while we plot your reply to your man."

"Can we order some margarita mix to add to these drinks, though?"

"Mine is growing on me, but we'll hook you up." Lyra headed over to the room phone to order up some goodies.

Amy gazed out over the porch, to the ocean beyond. She knew her heart would recover if she gave Vincent another chance, and she realized she wanted him in her life, at least for now. He was trying to make things work, and she was free to end it if this was the last chance. Maybe they could talk on the phone and he could tell her the truth, now, before she let her imagination carry her away.

*

Well, that was unexpected, Amy thought to herself as she hung up. And now she understood why Vincent was so unpredictable. It hadn't been about her at all.

She dipped a salty chip into the fresh guacamole, enjoying the creaminess, the fresh chopped jalapeno, and the satisfying crunch at the end. She chased it with a small sip of the ice cold margarita the waitstaff had brought up to the room, then slid into the plunge pool. My, this was the way all news should be delivered. With an ocean view and the right refreshments, any conversation was easier.

Lyra would be back in a few minutes. She was picking up some supplies from the lobby and chatting with the concierge, to give Amy a little space for what might have been a difficult phone call.

Amy dried herself off and relaxed in the chaise by the plunge pool. When Lyra returned with some papers and a shopping bag, Amy launched into the story.

"His story made total sense!"

"Fabulous. What is it? Or was it?"

"He didn't tell me because he didn't feel like it was his place to go into detail, but apparently his brother is an addict, and he relapsed around Thanksgiving."

"Oh no. That's tough, I'm sorry."

"It gets worse. Apparently, the parents have gone no-contact with the brother because he spent most of their retirement savings. And *then* his brother showed up at the house, on who-knows-what, on Christmas Eve."

"Oh my gosh, that's so stressful. I can see why he bailed. But why wouldn't he tell you then?"

"He told me he could barely see straight from panic and was totally overwhelmed. He also said that he took one look at me, sipping cocoa by the fire and getting excited about Christmas, and felt like he was on a different planet from me. He couldn't drag me into his family drama only to leave."

"But you would have helped him! And you're so understanding."

"Right? I *know*. But he didn't know what to think, or say, or do in the moment. He panicked and bailed. Which I can understand."

"He has to open up, though. This is all him being like, I don't know, a clam." Lyra still didn't look convinced. "A sexy, manly, tall…clam. You need a—a thing that's open. An oyster."

Amy thought about this briefly. "You're right. And I'm just going to wear myself out if there are too many chances. When I look at it though, it's been a couple of weeks. And I ask myself, maybe I need to give him a chance after the holidays, when life is at a normal pace, and we can just talk about normal things and see how we get along."

Lyra nodded. "That's so mature! I love it. Because you're right. You know he's awesome for the most part. Right? And he is interested in you, clearly. But you haven't been together in normal life very much. You deserve the chance to be normal." She picked up her drink and took a sip, then grabbed a few chips to nibble.

"Okay, then it's settled. More chances, more normal life, give it a couple of months. See if he opens up." Amy felt amenable to this as a solution. Lyra was right, it did seem like a mature relationship decision. She wasn't being reactive, but she also had her limits.

"Yes!" Lyra reached in for a hug. "Oh gosh, Amy, I hope it works out. I really want it to, for you."

They clinked glasses, Amy tearing up a bit at the choice. "In the meantime, I think we should be totally decadent, and consume all the things, and see all the things, and maybe send him a naughty text while we're out!"

Lyra held up her palm for a high-five. "That's my girl! I knew I taught you well."

"What did you pick up?" Amy noticed the unopened bag Lyra had set down.

She pulled out what looked like a tangle of colorful strings holding together some fabric.

"Matching bikinis!"

Amy spat out her drink. "I'm sorry, what now?"

*

The next days were perfect, even with the absurd matching bikinis that Lyra posted all over her social media. Amy didn't mind too much. She knew that someday she wouldn't be comfortable in something that revealing, and Vincent had loved the photo she had sent him of herself by the pool. Lyra definitely knew how to take a good photo, he had said during their new nightly bedtime talk.

"Hey, and you're a real photographer, so that's quite a compliment."

"It's true—but I vastly prefer home staging and landscapes to portraits. Sorry. Every girl I've dated has been a bit let down by the fact that there aren't a million stunning photos of us."

"Well thank you for disappointing me early on so I can recover." She hoped she sounded flirty.

"I aim to displease." He joked back.

"I can't believe we're leaving tomorrow, though."

"You can't live on tequila and chips, Amy."

"We ate real food! I had ceviche for dinner tonight, and huevos rancheros at brunch."

"That counts, okay. What time do you want me to pick you up at the airport?"

"Oh, I drove, but—wait, you're coming up?"

"Sure, it's New Year's. I have a few more days before my next shoot. That is, if you'd like to see me. I can get a room in town if you need."

She smiled to herself and replied. "That won't be necessary. I think. I should be there by around eight."

"That sounds good to me. I'll make sure I bring a few groceries, too."

"Well, there's a key sitting on top of the door frame. Make sure you check on the cats!"

He chuckled. "Yes, ma'am, I will. Safe travels. Can't wait to make up with you." His voice deepened suggestively.

"Me neither. Sweet dreams." She ended the call, still grinning, and set down the phone.

Lyra looked at her. "Amy! I can feel that chemistry through the phone. You *have* to try it with this guy. Conrad was never like this and you were together for *years*." She had a point.

Amy nodded. "If this works, it will work better than anything."

*

The next night, Amy took the familiar lakeside road back to the cottage. The Christmas-fueled energy had dissipated somewhat, but she was still in good spirits. She pulled into her parking space, right beside Vincent. She could see the lights of the cottage below.

Amy grabbed her weekend bag and descended the stairs slowly. She had arrived with Larry and was coming home to an intriguing man who wanted to be with her, and two cats who were sweetly bonded together. Getting away had helped her clear her head, but she still felt a little nervous about seeing Vincent after all of the emotional charge of the last few days.

She opened the door and entered. "I'm here!"

Larry and Midnight were waiting at the door. Vincent stood up from the sofa, crossed in front of the roaring fire he had built, and took Amy into his arms. He leaned down with a welcoming kiss. She returned the gesture, reaching up behind his neck to draw him in more closely.

He led her by the hand to the sofa, where he had a cup of tea waiting for her. "I poured it when I heard you pull up," he said. They cozied up together, enjoying the other's proximity, breathing easily and holding one another.

"I'm so glad we are trying together."

He sighed softly. "I'm so grateful for you. Thank you—just tell me if my communication is weird. And I'll be working on making it better too, obviously."

"You know, it isn't obvious," Amy mused. "A lot of men just direct women on how to make room for them. You're not like that because you work to make things better."

"I hope so." He kissed the top of her head. "I did one thing while you were gone to make things better."

She liked the sound of this. "Oh yeah, what was that?"

"I have two more jobs in this area by the lake right after the new year. And I may have made a few calls to a friend in South Florida about referrals in the Miami area. You'll have to check my recent calls to see, though." He winked, grinning.

Amy caught her breath. "Really?"

He caught up her hand. "I figure if we give this a chance, we should really give it a chance."

She smiled. "Yes, I like that idea." She noticed a little gift bag on the table. "Hey, what's this?"

"That might be for you. A belated Christmas present."

She smiled, "I wondered if there was something."

"There was, but I was going to show you the picture and make it a rain check because I couldn't get it here in time, and then I just, well, you know the rest."

He handed her the gift and watched her open it. Inside was a pair of earrings: each earring was a double hoop of white and gold. She'd noticed a three-hoop, tricolor pair while they were watching a jewelry ad on TV. At the time, she'd commented that she liked the style, but didn't wear rose gold. He'd noticed, and found what she liked, and remembered.

Amy leaned in to kiss Vincent. "These are perfect. Thank you."

He relaxed. Apparently he had been a little nervous about his gift. "Are they what you wanted? I went with the 18-karat gold because it looked a little more refined, a little more special."

She nodded, excited. "Yes! That is perfect. You have excellent taste." They kissed and Amy paused to try on her new earrings. "How do I look?"

"Gorgeous. Merry Christmas." Vincent took her hand and kissed it.

Just then, as if on cue, Larry and Midnight climbed up for pets. Amy had Midnight nuzzling up by her face, Larry making biscuits on her lap, and Vincent holding her hand. "This is quite a family we're turning out to be."

"I hate to break it to you, Amy, but everyone seems to love you." He gave her hand a gentle, extra squeeze.

"Everyone, huh?" she teased, smiling at him.

"Yes," he admitted. "Everyone. Including me." And he leaned in for another kiss.

THE END

Volume II of the series available Winter 2022.